TRADEWIND BOOKS

THE EMERALD CURSE

Born and raised in Britain, Canadian writer Simon Rose lives in Calgary, Alberta. His first novel, *The Alchemist's Portrait*, was published by Tradewind Books in 2003. *The Sorcerer's Letterbox*, published by Tradewind Books in 2004, was shortlisted for both the Silver Birch and the Diamond Willow awards. His latest book, *The Clone Conspiracy*, was published by Tradewind Books in 2005.

THE EMERALD CURSE

THE EMERALD CURSE

BY SIMON ROSE

ILLUSTRATIONS BY CYNTHIA NUGENT

VANCOUVER   LONDON

This book is dedicated to Sam and Georgia,
who make it all worthwhile.
- S.R.

Published in Canada and the UK by Tradewind Books Ltd.
www.tradewindbooks.com

Distribution in the UK by Turnaround
www.turnaround-uk.com

Text copyright © 2006 by Simon Rose
Cover and interior illustrations © 2006 by Cynthia Nugent
Book design by Jacqueline Wang

Printed in Canada on Ancient Forest Friendly paper
10 9 8 7 6 5 4 3 2 1

Cataloguing-in-Publication Data for this book available from the British Library.

Library and Archives Canada Cataloguing in Publication

Rose, Simon, 1961-
    The emerald curse / by Simon Rose.

ISBN 1-896580-90-4

    1. Comic books, strips, etc.--Juvenile fiction. I. Title.

PS8585.O7335E44 2006   jC813'.6   C2006-901887-1

The publisher thanks the Canada
Council for the Arts for its support.

 Canada Council **Conseil des Arts**
for the Arts **du Canada**

The publisher also wishes to thank the Government
of British Columbia for the financial support it
has extended through the book publishing tax credit
program and the British Columbia Arts Council.

 BRITISH COLUMBIA ARTS COUNCIL

The publisher also acknowledges the financial support of the Government of
Canada through the Book Publishing Industry Development Program (BPIDP)
and the Association for the Export of Canadian Books.

CONTENTS

CHAPTER ONE

BREAKING THE CONTRACT

Ever since he was a small boy, Charles Kelly had dreamt of being a comic-book artist. Although he had many wonderful ideas for stories, he lacked artistic talent. Simply put, he couldn't draw.

When he was a young university student in London, Kelly often visited antique markets. One day, while rummaging through an assortment of objects at one of the stalls, he discovered an antique fountain pen with a small green gemstone embedded in its barrel. The stallholder smiled broadly as he recounted a fabulous story about the pen and its mysterious jewel. The gemstone had been stolen from a treasure hoard unearthed during the excavation of ancient Troy in the early 1870s. The stone was then smuggled to England, where it was used to decorate a fountain pen specially commissioned by one Alastair Grenville, a book illustrator in Victorian London. For a few brief years, Grenville enjoyed phenomenal success. There were persistent rumours in the artistic community that his good fortune was due to the remarkable pen that he used to create his artwork. One evening in the spring of 1877, the stallholder explained, Grenville mysteriously disappeared without a trace.

Although Kelly strongly suspected the man's story was designed to sweeten the sale, he bought the antique pen. Some weeks later, Kelly used the pen to doodle on a scrap of paper, absentmindedly rubbing the pen's jewel with his thumb as he drew. He was astonished to see a powerful drawing of a hideous face.

"I must be dreaming," Kelly thought to himself.

He then heard a strange voice inside his head. "This is no dream, Charles Kelly. I have been watching you ever since you bought that pen. My name is Karakor, and I can transform your dream of becoming a famous comic-book artist into reality."

"How do you know about my dream?" Kelly demanded.

"I know you better than you know yourself."

Kelly thought for a moment. "What do I have to do?"

"All you have to do is create a story where evil decisively triumphs over good," Karakor explained. "If you agree, I will grant you the artistic talent necessary to guarantee your success. From that point on, you will discover that you have the ability to draw all the wonderful stories swirling around in your head. But you must use the antique pen. If you do this, your achievements will exceed your wildest dreams."

"What's the catch?" asked Kelly.

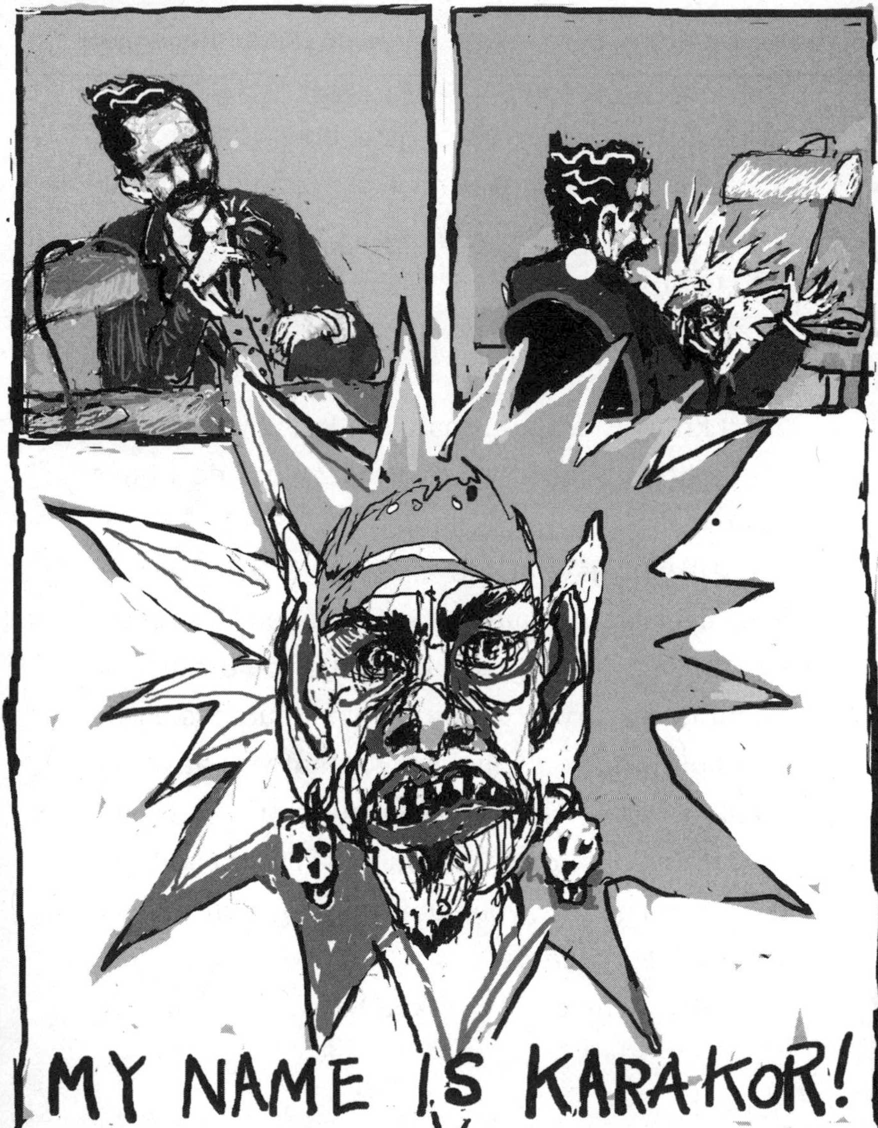
MY NAME IS KARAKOR!

"There is no catch," Karakor answered. "It's as simple as that. That's all you need to do. I'll make you rich and famous."

"It doesn't feel right," said Kelly. "I just don't know."

"You disappoint me, Kelly," said Karakor. "I thought you had more ambition."

The face on the page started to disappear.

"Wait," said Kelly, hurriedly. "I agree."

"You agree to my terms?"

"Yes," said Kelly, solemnly.

"You must write the story I have requested by midnight on your sixtieth birthday," Karakor added. "If you do not, you will wish you had never been born. Do we have a deal?"

"We do," said Kelly.

The face on the paper slowly faded away until only the blank page remained.

Within a year, Charles Kelly had acquired a reputation as one of the world's greatest comic-book artists. His comics went on to win awards around the globe. Kelly moved to New York and bought a large old house on Long Island. He built a studio in the attic, where he continued to work for decades.

Charles Kelly's sixtieth birthday came and went. He felt relieved that Karakor had not returned as he had promised, and was convinced that the demon had forgotten their contract. One morning, he sat down at his easel beside the attic window, briefly glancing at the sailboats in the distance. He picked up the antique pen and began to sketch the figure of the Speck, one of his many superhero characters. But when Kelly looked down at his drawing, the hideous face of Karakor stared back at him.

Kelly abruptly stood up, stepping away from the easel. For a moment, the attic was deathly quiet. Then Kelly heard the ominous voice of the demon rattling in his head.

"The time has come," said Karakor. "You have failed to honour our agreement."

"No, I haven't," Kelly insisted. "I created the story you wanted."

"Then where is it?" Karakor demanded.

"Right here," said Kelly, picking up an oversized pad of paper. "I finished it last month. It's an extra-long story called *The Eclipse of the Superheroes.*"

"What good is it to me sitting here in your studio?" snapped Karakor. "I want the whole world to read it. When will it be published?"

"Never!" said Kelly defiantly. "It doesn't have to be published. That wasn't the deal. All I had to do was to create the story, and I did."

Karakor flew into a rage. "I gave you everything!" he roared. "You would have nothing without me. Nothing! Your artwork, your success, your acclaim are all my doing! I'll tear you apart!"

"I'm not afraid of you," said Kelly, his voice shaking. "You can't kill me. I've fulfilled our pact."

Karakor glared coldly.

"Perhaps I won't kill you," he declared, "but, as I promised, you will wish that you had never been born!"

Kelly tried to back away but found to his horror that he couldn't move his legs. "What are you doing?" he exclaimed, as he was steadily pulled toward his easel. He tried to shout for help, but no sound came from his lips.

Charles Kelly vanished.

CHAPTER TWO

KELLY'S CLASSIC COMICS

As his dad turned onto Bayshore Drive, Sam took out his pocket sketchpad and began to draw a picture of the sea, speckled with sailboats. Sam's grandfather, the famous comic-book creator Charles Kelly, had mysteriously disappeared two years earlier. Although no body had been found, Kelly was presumed dead. Sam's mother, Diana, had taken possession of Kelly's Long Island house, and Sam was excited to be moving in. He liked the tree-lined streets, luxurious cars, perfectly manicured lawns and elegant homes of Upton Beach.

Finally, the car came to a halt outside his grandfather's house. Since Charles Kelly's sudden disappearance, his former home had fallen into disrepair. The front yard was totally overgrown, and the paint was peeling on the front door and on all the window frames.

"The old place could do with a good clean-up," said Sam's dad, Mike, as he lifted out the luggage.

"We certainly have a lot of work to do," Sam's mum agreed, grabbing a suitcase and walking up the front path to the house. Sam followed closely behind, carrying his sketchpad and a small bag. When he walked through the front door, he was pleased to see that the house looked exactly as he had remembered it. An old brass lantern rested on a small table just inside the doorway, and an antique rug his grandfather had bought on a trip to Turkey stretched along the narrow entry that led to the front stairway. An ornately framed oil painting of Sam's grandmother, who had died before he was born, hung on the wall.

"I think I'll go and take a look around," said Sam, clutching his sketchpad.

"Take your bag upstairs first," said his dad. "You're in the same room that you used to stay in when you came to visit Granddad."

"The Nelsons will be here around seven for a barbeque," his mother added, "and they're looking forward to finally meeting you. You're okay for half an hour or so. We'll give you a call when they get here."

"Sounds good," said Sam.

Sam tossed his bag onto the bed, crossed the landing and climbed the narrow, winding staircase that led to his grandfather's studio. The attic hadn't been touched since Charles Kelly had disappeared. The walls were covered in posters depicting the covers of some of his award-winning comics. There were many framed pictures of his grandfather holding trophies and awards. Some of these same trophies were scattered around the room, now simply gathering dust. Sam had been

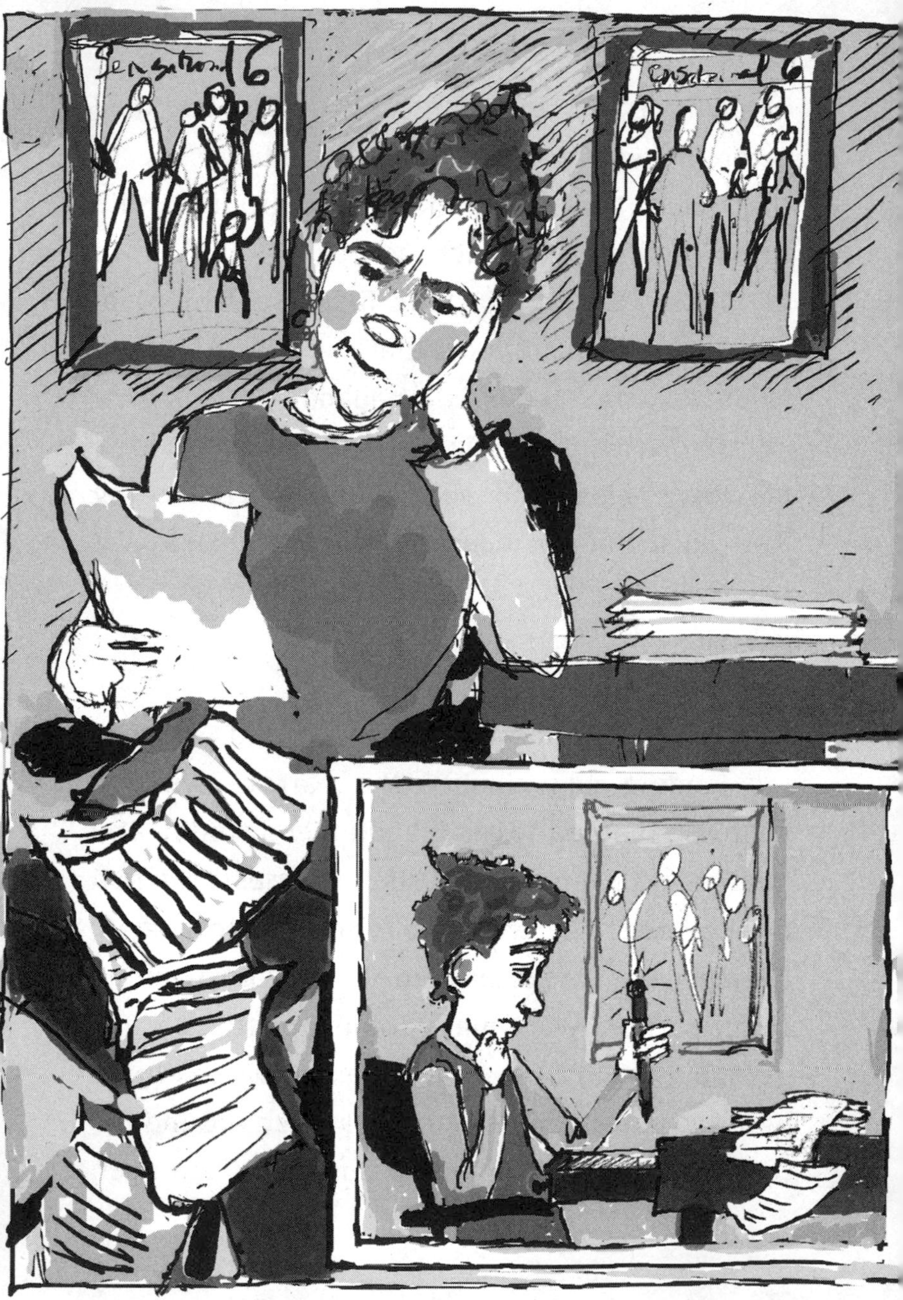

told he had a great talent for art and illustration, but doubted if he would ever be able to match his grandfather's level of success. Charles Kelly was considered the greatest comic-book artist of all time.

Beside the window stood a tall stool next to an easel. On the floor, almost hidden behind a bureau, Sam saw a thick pad of paper, the same kind that Kelly had used to produce his work. Sam picked it up and flipped over the pages. He was thrilled to see that it was a complete unpublished comic that he had never seen before. It was an adventure featuring Kelly's most famous superhero team, the Sensational Six, and guest-starring all the other superheroes that Kelly had created. As Sam flicked through the pages, however, his initial excitement turned to disappointment. The story was about the victory of Baron Midnight, the Sensational Six's archenemy, who used a machine called the ContraRay to banish all of Kelly's superheroes to an alternate universe known as ContraRealm. At the story's conclusion, Midnight became master of the world.

The comic was terrible, and Sam could understand why his grandfather had never published it.

Sam turned his attention to his grandfather's desk. The desk diary was still open to Thursday, August 15th, exactly two years earlier. Attached to the edge of the desk was an old-fashioned pencil sharpener. There was an empty inkpot and a chipped mug filled with pencils and pens. The desk's in-tray was devoid of papers, but a wooden rack attached to the wall contained a stack of comic books.

Sam sat down at the desk. He pulled open the right-hand drawer and found an old-fashioned pen with a green gemstone embedded in its barrel.

CHAPTER THREE

Sam picked up the pen and turned it over in his hand. It looked very old and certainly didn't seem like the kind of thing his grandfather would have used for drawing. He put it down and turned his attention to the stack of comics. The first one he pulled out was issue 9 of *The Sword of Borak*. This series featured the adventures of a warrior who lived in a time before recorded history. Sam had read all the Borak stories over and over and knew their plots inside out. He particularly admired issue 9's illustrations, so typical of his grandfather's work. In the story, the evil warlock

Velaron had finally located a mystical emerald designed to open a portal to other worlds. The cover showed Velaron standing triumphantly before the pulsating jewel, declaring, "At last it is mine!" Behind Velaron, Borak emerged from the shadows with his sword drawn. *The Sword of Borak* was one of Kelly's less popular creations. The series ran for only nine issues and was quickly forgotten.

Sam then pulled out an issue of *The Speck.* In that series, Byron Castlemaine, a mild-mannered scientist, took on the alter ego of a shrinking superhero, the Speck, to fight crime. Byron Castlemaine was a multi-millionaire, with a secret underground laboratory hidden deep beneath his mansion. On the comic's cover, the Speck hid behind a small radio, eavesdropping while a group of men seated at a table were counting out the proceeds from a recent bank robbery.

Sam then spotted his all-time favourite comic, issue 55 of *The Sensational Six*, Kelly's most successful superhero team. Under the leadership of the Golden Guardian, the members of the

Sensational Six included the Titan; Supernova; the winged Redhawk; SynthoLord, the shape-shifting android; and Psychic Girl. Golden Guardian concealed his true identity behind a helmet and mask and wore a suit of gleaming armour crammed with weapons of every description. The rest of the team all wore similar black leather uniforms, complete with the famous number six in a white hexagon on the left side of the chest. The Sensational Six had many deadly enemies, but their most frequent adversary was the sinister Baron Midnight. Every five or six issues, the baron would develop a nefarious scheme to take over the world, only to be ultimately thwarted by the team. Entitled "The Fortress of Baron Midnight," the story in issue 55 took place at the baron's stronghold deep in the mountains. This was where the baron had succeeded in breeding his monstrous hybrids, combinations of the most vicious and terrifying animals and insects on earth. They formed a formidable army loyal only to the baron.

The comic's cover was the most spectacular Sam had ever seen. The baron's multi-towered castle with its whitewashed walls and red-tiled roofs was in the background. The grey skull with bat wings that served as Baron Midnight's symbol was prominently displayed on flags flying from the battlements. At the front gates stood Baron Midnight in his black armour, metal mask and flowing red cape, exhorting his guards and hybrids to attack the Sensational Six. At the baron's side stood the Scorplion, which had the head and body of a lion but a scorpion's tail and pincers. Racing toward the advancing heroes was the Waspilla, possessing the body of a gorilla, claws the length of steak knives and the head and stinger of a wasp. The Titan was already locked in battle with the Crocbear, comprising a crocodile's head, a bear's body and a long reptilian tail armed with deadly spikes. In the sky above the fortress, duelling with Golden Guardian and Redhawk, flew the Airserpent, which had the heads of two cobras on the body of an eagle. The cover was bursting with action, and Sam remembered that the story inside the comic had certainly lived up to expectations. It was perhaps Charles Kelly's greatest ever adventure.

Sam then remembered another reason he had always treasured *Sensational Six* #55. It was the only comic where Charles Kelly had included his own likeness in one of the panels. Sam quickly flicked through the pages and soon located the cameo picture of his grandfather. Baron Midnight's fortress was situated high on a craggy hilltop overlooking a valley dotted with tiny alpine villages. Sure enough, halfway through the story, Charles Kelly's face appeared as one of the villagers. Taking out his sketchpad, Sam decided to copy the panel. He grabbed the old pen from the drawer and idly sketched the image of Charles Kelly. Then he noticed that the jewel on the pen's barrel started to glow slightly as he drew. Suddenly, something took control of his hand, and Sam found himself drawing a word balloon above the face he had just completed. He was then shocked to see his hand use the pen to write words in the balloon.

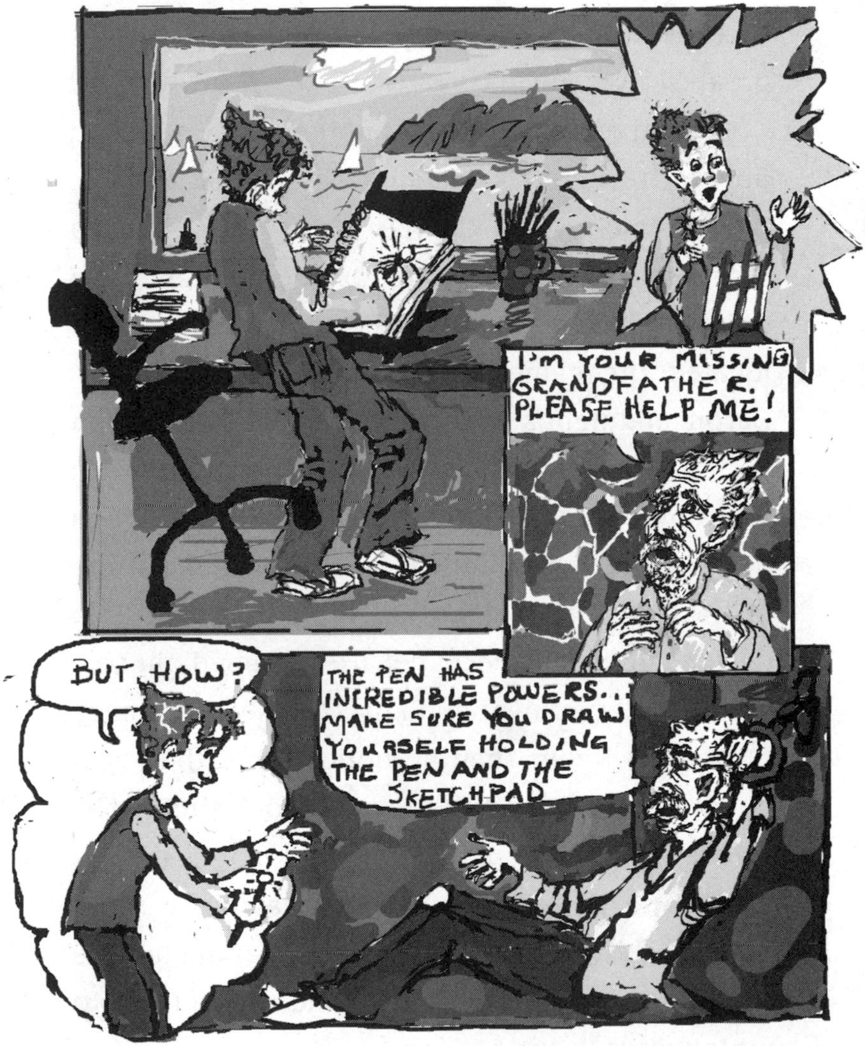
I'M YOUR MISSING GRANDFATHER. PLEASE HELP ME!
BUT HOW?
THE PEN HAS INCREDIBLE POWERS... MAKE SURE YOU DRAW YOURSELF HOLDING THE PEN AND THE SKETCHPAD

Get me outta here! it read.

Before he knew what was happening, Sam found himself compelled to draw another panel on the sketchpad, this time containing his own image. His hand then scrawled, *Who are you?* in a word balloon above his own picture.

The jewel on the pen began to glow brightly as Sam's hand drew another likeness of his grandfather. This time, the word balloon read: *I'm your grandfather. I'm trapped in my own comic book universe, a prisoner in Baron Midnight's fortress. Please help me.*

Sam flipped to another page on his sketchpad and quickly drew himself again. *But how?*

The pen has incredible powers. You can use it to get here.

I don't understand.

The pen in Sam's hand immediately completed another balloon beside his grandfather's likeness and urgently scratched out instructions.

You need to draw yourself inside a panel from The Sensational Six. *Make sure you draw yourself holding the pen and sketchpad.*

Sam regained control of his own hand as the jewel on the pen stopped glowing. There were no further messages.

CHAPTER FOUR

PIECES OF
THE PUZZLE

"Sam! The Nelsons are here," his father bellowed from the bottom of the stairs.

Sam was still stunned by what he had seen. It took him a moment to answer.

"Sam!" his father called again.

"Okay," he shouted back. "I'll be right down."

Sam considered telling his parents what had happened, but he wasn't sure how he would ever explain it. They might even think he was crazy. Putting down the old pen, he raced downstairs.

Through the sliding doors, Sam could see Mr. and Mrs. Nelson, the neighbours, chatting with

23

his mother on the patio. Sam's dad was busy at the barbecue.

"Here he is," exclaimed Mr. Nelson, as Sam walked onto the patio. "Why, you're the image of Charles."

"He's not bad at drawing, either," added Sam's dad with a grin, as he flipped the burgers.

"So, you're following in your grandfather's footsteps?" Mrs. Nelson asked.

Sam felt a shiver run down his spine.

"I dunno," said Sam, with a shrug. "Maybe."

"Don't be so modest," said his mother. "You're a brilliant artist. It's not just us. Everyone says how good you are."

"Is my hamburger ready?" Sam asked, feeling uncomfortable.

"Right here," replied his dad. "Pass me your plate."

Sam wolfed down his dinner while the adults continued their conversation.

"So, Diana," Mr. Nelson asked, "the house is now officially yours?"

"Well, not really," replied Sam's mother, with a sigh. "The police think that my father must be dead, but the court can't officially declare it for another five years. I can't sell the house or anything like that. But we can live here and keep it in shape."

"The garden especially needs a lot of work," Mike added.

"Charles was going to do some landscaping," said Mr. Nelson. "We were discussing that only a couple of days before he disappeared."

"It was as if he'd simply vanished into thin air," Mrs. Nelson remembered. "The coffee pot was still full. There were even dishes in the sink."

"That fits with what the detectives told us," said Diana.

Sam thought again about telling his parents what he had experienced in the attic, but immediately thought better of it. He wanted to work out what it all meant.

"Excuse me," said Sam, "but I think I'll head up to my room."

"No dessert?" his mother asked him.

"I'm really not that hungry," said Sam. "I think I'll just go and read for a while."

"Leave us boring grownups to our chatter, eh?" Mr. Nelson asked, sounding amused.

Sam didn't go to his bedroom, but headed straight to the attic. Once in the studio, Sam took the antique pen out of the drawer. The gemstone in the barrel immediately began to glow. He began to copy a panel from *The Sensational Six* #55 onto his sketchpad, depicting the baron's mountain fortress. Sam's version had a crucial difference: he included a representation of himself, hidden in the woods outside the baron's stronghold. The instant Sam put the finishing touches to the drawing, the jewel on the pen suddenly glowed even brighter. As Sam brushed it with his thumb, the attic dissolved around him.

CHAPTER FIVE

THE FORTRESS OF BARON MIDNIGHT

Sam couldn't believe his eyes. He was standing in the woods on a mountainside, staring up at the stone walls and red-tiled roofs of Baron Midnight's fortress. The familiar batwinged skull emblem adorned the many flags billowing in the breeze. The huge building with its six imposing towers looked exactly the same as it did in the comics. The tall central tower with its solitary window was where the baron imprisoned his most-hated enemies. Known as Skull Tower, it housed the cells where Baron Midnight had banished his own father years before, leaving him

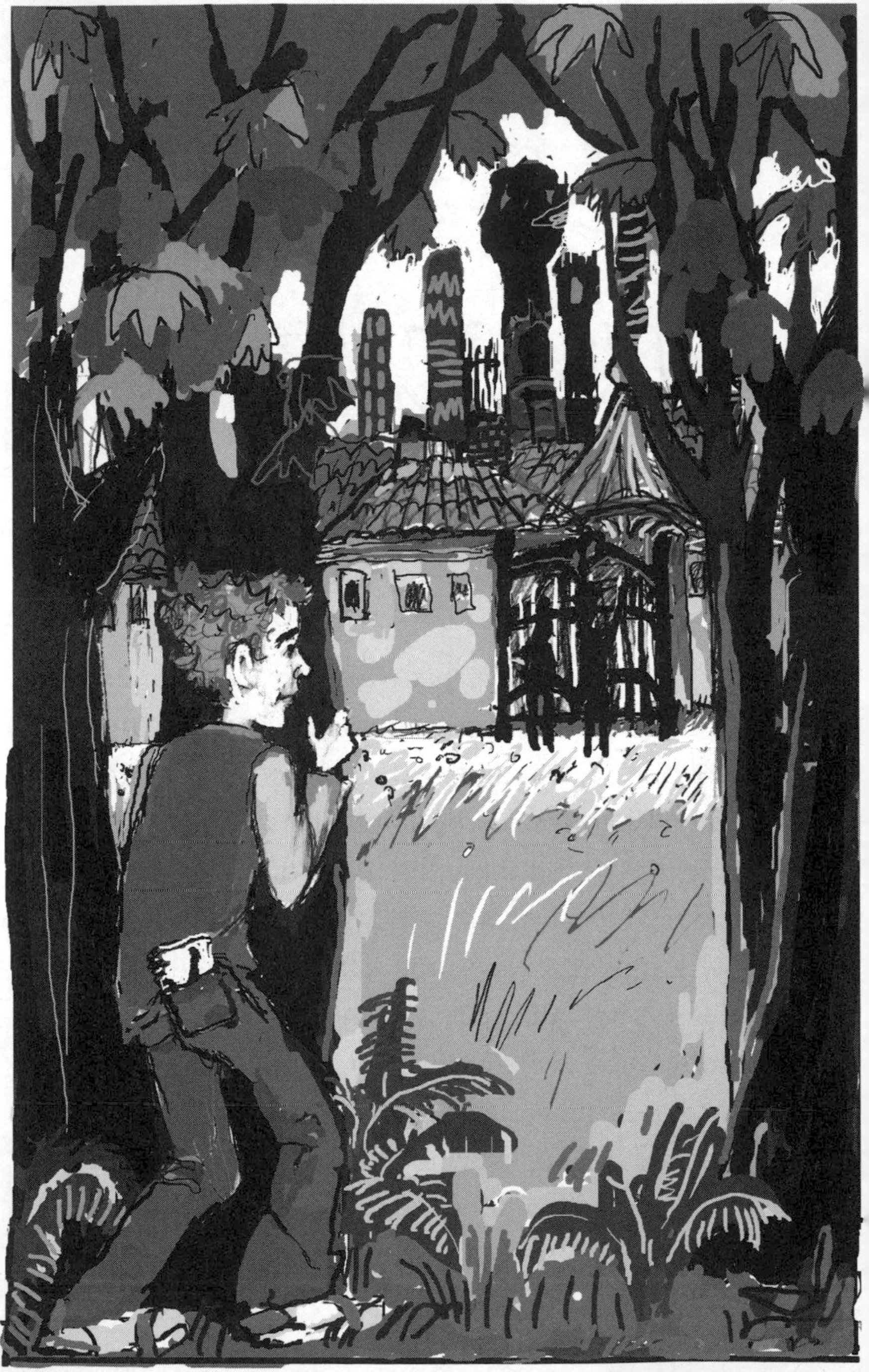

to die of starvation. To the left was the shorter Dome Tower, housing the baron's laboratory, where he conducted his experiments and created his hybrids. The two front iron gates were the only perceivable entrance to the inner compound.

Sam scanned the skies, looking for signs of the heroes, but all he saw were plumes of smoke rising from the valley below. A noise caught Sam's attention. He quietly backed away into the woods where he would not be seen. A group of men and women emerged from the forest. Some were dressed in combat fatigues, others in peasant clothing. They carried a variety of weapons—some had assault guns, automatic rifles and machine pistols while others were armed with antique hunting rifles or handguns.

At first it wasn't clear who was in charge, then Sam saw that a young woman, probably in her mid-twenties, was giving everyone instructions. She was tall and slim, with closely cropped black hair. As she neared his hiding place, Sam couldn't help but notice the intensity of her gaze. As the woman looked out toward Baron Midnight's fortress, a young man with long dark hair tied in a ponytail approached her.

They were soon joined by an older man with a beard, carrying a weapon that resembled a rocket launcher. The bearded man crouched down and laid the device on the ground. He pressed a button, and a computer keypad and small screen slid out from the side of the weapon. The man keyed in a code and nodded in satisfaction.

"Now remember," said the bearded man, "the codes to disable the lasers will only work once the cannons have been activated. You'll need to break cover, allow the fortress guards to see you, then wait for the first blast."

"Sounds dangerous," said the younger man.

"I know. But once they begin firing," the bearded man continued, "I'll aim the electro-disrupter. It will disable the cannons and scramble the entire defence system so we can attack."

"I'm still worried about the hybrids, Altina," said the younger man, turning to the woman.

"Our information has always been reliable, Andreas," the woman assured him. "Our brothers have engaged the baron's army in the Western Sector, and he'll have taken the hybrids there. We should be able to defeat Ragnor and his guards easily."

"Understood," Andreas nodded.

"Let's move out," said Altina.

Sam watched as the entire group moved into the open, in full view of the fortress. Immediately, alarms pierced the air. Sam watched in dismay as laser cannons blasted the hillside, forcing the ragtag army to take shelter. The bearded man aimed the electro-disrupter at the laser cannons. One by one, they fell silent, but not before a final blast rang out. Sam was shocked. Where the bearded man had stood, there was nothing but scorched earth.

From his hiding place, Sam watched a gruesome scene unfold. Altina encouraged her followers as they raced toward the fortress. Midnight's guards came rushing out through the gates, led by a tall, bespectacled man with a thin, black moustache. He was wearing the traditional jet-black uniform worn by Baron Midnight's army.

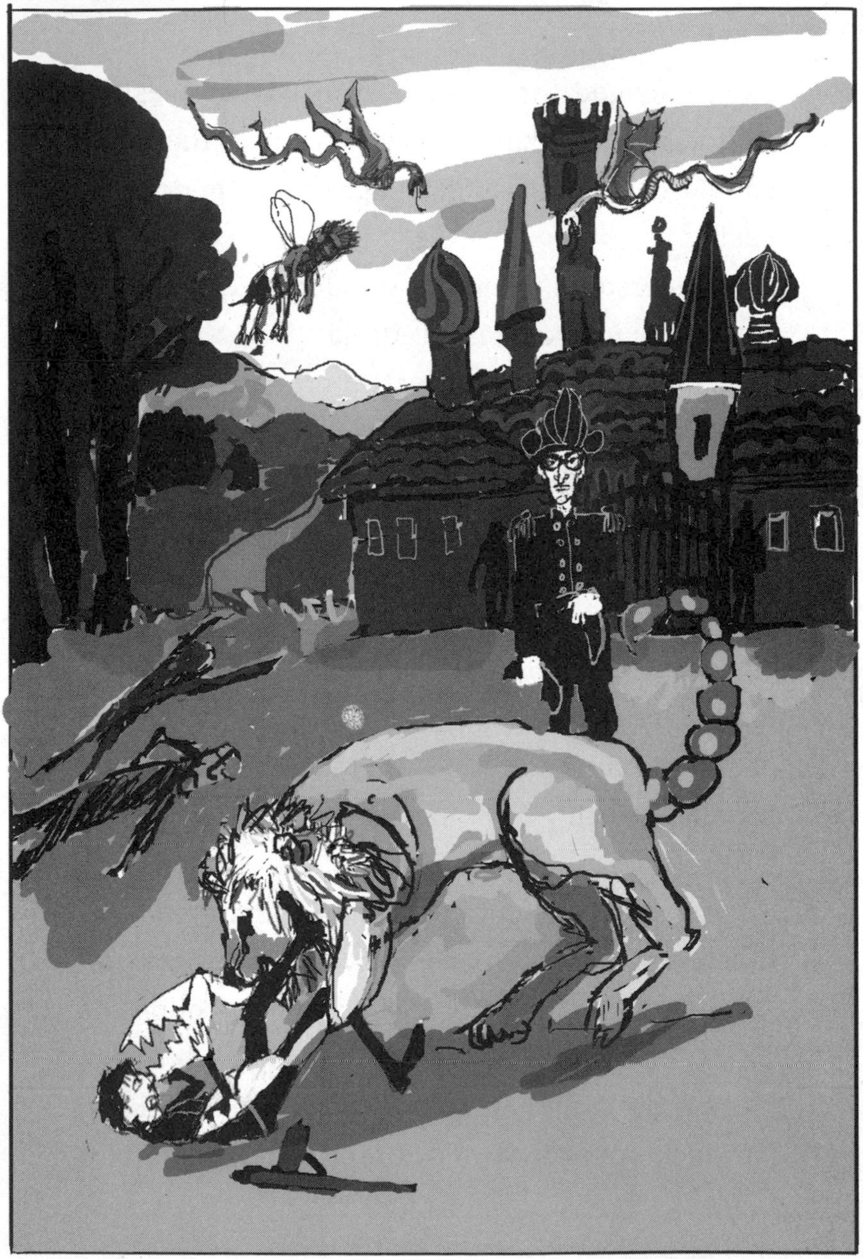

The upper sleeves of his uniform were decorated with armbands emblazoned with the baron's bat-winged skull emblem. Sam recognized the man as Ragnor, Baron Midnight's much-feared second-in-command.

To Sam's horror, a clutch of hybrids roared out from behind the fortress walls. Sam had seen the grotesque hybrids countless times as comic illustrations, but it was terrifying to see them in real life. Each one combined the most lethal and ferocious elements of animals and insects. They were hideous. The onrushing hybrids easily overwhelmed the attackers. Two Airserpents circled overhead, repeatedly swooping down on the fighters. Grasping them in their talons, the huge monsters then soared away and flung their victims to their deaths.

Sam watched as other hybrids rushed out to join the battle. A fearsome Crocbear lumbered down the hillside. It seized one man in its powerful jaws while effortlessly tossing others aside with a sweep of its spiked tail. Alongside the Crocbear, a Hyenagator, one of Baron Midnight's newest creations, snapped and snarled at the fighters. The remaining attackers were holding their own against Baron Midnight's forces, until a Scorpion charged, killing every rebel in its path. It pounced on Altina, pinning her firmly to the ground with its huge pincers. As the Scorpion raised its stinger, Altina's weapon fell from her hand. When it hit the ground, it fired in Sam's direction. A huge tree branch fell, missing Sam by inches. When Sam was able to turn his attention back to the battlefield, he saw the attackers retreating in disarray, with Ragnor's forces in hot pursuit.

Sam waited until the guards and hybrids disappeared from view before leaving his hiding place. He felt sick at what he had witnessed but knew that he had to get inside the fortress to rescue his grandfather.

Suddenly, he heard a low buzzing sound. He saw to his horror that two Waspillas were hovering above the trees. The monsters were darting back and forth, making a clicking sound as they surveyed the woods below with their large insect eyes. Sam held his breath and thought that his heart was going to burst. All of a sudden the Waspillas turned and flew away.

Sam brushed the leaves from his clothes. He crept to the edge of the woods and gazed up at the fortress. He quickly realized that the main gates had been left open. Here was his chance!

Sam ran toward the fortress. When he reached the gates, he quickly slipped inside and darted across the inner courtyard. He shrank back into the shadows beneath a staircase and could see Skull Tower looming above him. Sam figured it was a good place to start looking for his grandfather. He closed his eyes and tried to remember the exact location of the entrance. Just then, he was grabbed from behind, and a hand was clamped over his mouth.

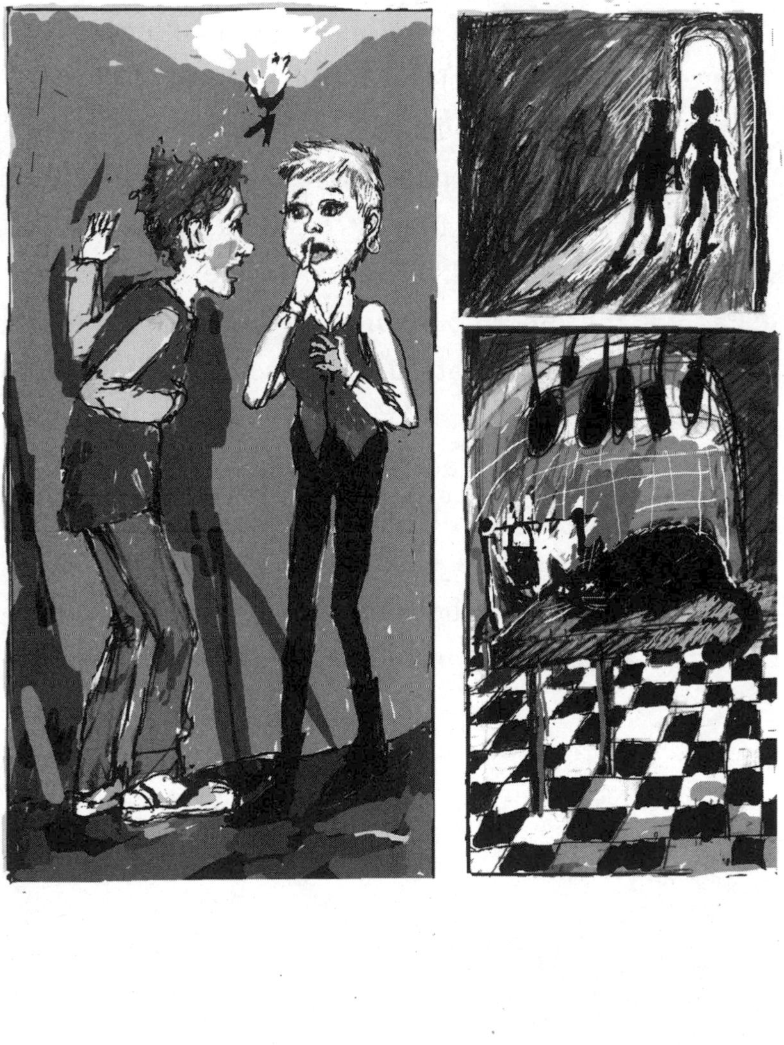

CHAPTER SIX

TWISTED FICTION

Sam's first thought was that Baron Midnight's guards had caught him, but he relaxed as he heard a whispered "shush" and found himself being gently pulled back deeper into the shadows. When he was able to turn around, Sam found himself face to face with a girl dressed in dark pants, a white shirt and a dark leather vest. As his eyes adjusted to the semi-darkness, Sam saw that she had bright blue eyes and short blond hair. He recognized her as Tanya, Baron Midnight's only daughter. He was about to speak when she put a finger to her lips.

"We're not safe here," Tanya whispered. "Follow me."

Sam wondered if he could trust her but quickly realized that he had no choice. He followed her through a nearby doorway and along a dimly lit corridor.

"My father's away," said Tanya, as they reached the kitchen, "and the servants won't be back until morning. We won't be disturbed in here."

The kitchen was enormous. Over the large fireplace hung pots, pans, skillets, ladles and other cooking utensils. Sam noticed a black cat lying on the long wooden table in the centre of the kitchen.

"Shoo, Cole!" Tanya ordered, as she brushed the cat off the table.

With a disgruntled meow, Cole darted out of the room.

Tanya settled onto one of the surrounding stools, gesturing to a seat opposite her.

"Who are you?" Tanya asked. "You're from the world outside, aren't you?"

"Yes," replied Sam, feeling very uneasy.

"You must be Charles Kelly's grandson!" Tanya blurted out. "Sam—it *is* Sam, isn't it?"

"How do you know about us?" Sam asked, surprised.

"I was there at your grandfather's interrogation. My father's spies told him about the arrival of a mysterious stranger in one of the villages," Tanya explained. "My father was concerned that he might be connected with the rebels. The next day, my father's men found him. Your grandfather tried to run, but he was quickly captured and brought to the fortress."

"Did Baron Midnight know who my grandfather was?"

"Not at first," Tanya replied, "but my father used the HypnoRay to probe his mind. He was amazed to discover that he had captured the creator of the very world we live in. That's how I know about you. Under the influence of the HypnoRay, he talked about the things that mattered to him, the people he cared about. He kept mentioning your name." She paused for a second. "Did you come here to try and take him back to your world? Do you have a plan? I'll help you get back to your own world, but you have to help us first."

"Maybe we could get help from the Sensational Six," Sam suggested.

"They're gone, Sam," said Tanya, flatly. "All the heroes are gone."

"What do you mean?" asked Sam, taken aback.

"They've been cast into ContraRealm by my father."

"ContraRealm!" said Sam. His mind raced back to the unpublished comic he had seen in the attic.

So the heroes are all trapped. That's why they didn't come to the rescue of the rebels, he thought.

"With the heroes gone," Tanya explained, "my father's power became unstoppable, and it turned him into a sadistic monster. After discovering that some nearby villages were linked to the resistance, he ordered them erased from the map. You saw the plumes of smoke in the valley? All the townspeople—men, women, children and even animals—were slaughtered and the villages razed to the ground as if they had never existed."

"That's horrific!" He thought for a moment about the poor villagers and the hopelessness of their situation.

"Our people live in fear. Those who dare to join or help the resistance are condemned to a life on the run. Their families are often eliminated as a lesson to others. My uncle Mathias led the resistance until he was killed a few months ago. My cousins are now in charge. When my mother tried to help them, she paid for it with her life."

"She betrayed your father?" Sam was shocked. Baron Midnight's wife, Anastasia, had always been extremely loyal, blind to her husband's evil.

"Yes, and my father killed her. He told me that my uncle had done it, but I knew the truth right away. You see, my mother was afraid. She told me that if anything happened to her, I was not to trust anything that my father said."

"Your mother was very brave," Sam said.

"Yes, and I've tried to honour her by carrying on her struggle. I've been working as a double agent for the rebels. My father sends me out to spy on their operations, but I've been feeding him false information."

"Tanya, what can I do to help?"

"First, we've got to free your grandfather. He's in a cell in Skull Tower," she said. "But the approach to his cell is protected by laser tripwires."

Sam thought for a moment. "I have an idea," he said. "In one of my grandfather's comics, there's a shrinking superhero character called the Speck. If he were here, he could slip under laser beams like that."

"But he's a prisoner in ContraRealm like the other superheroes," Tanya reminded him.

"I know," replied Sam, "but in order to shrink, the Speck used a special bracelet. Even if he's a prisoner, there would still be several spare ones in his laboratory."

"So?" asked Tanya.

"I should be able to get into the lab and grab a couple of his shrinking bracelets," Sam continued.

"But how?"

"The same way I got here," explained Sam. "I'll draw a picture of myself in a panel from a Speck story and I'll be transported there. Then I can use one bracelet to make myself as tiny as the Speck and go under the beams. I'll give the other bracelet to my grandfather, and we'll be able to escape together."

Sam pulled the sketchpad from his pocket and took out the antique pen. Working from memory, he sketched a picture of the Speck's subterranean headquarters. As Sam drew himself into the picture, the gemstone suddenly shone brightly. When he brushed the jewel with his thumb, Baron Midnight's fortress melted away.

CHAPTER SEVEN

SUBTERRANEAN SECRETS

Sam blinked, trying to adjust to the dim light in the underground laboratory. It was filled with scientific equipment, computers, forensic and analytical devices and a wide assortment of high-tech machinery. Away from the equipment area, scores of stalactites hung from the ceiling. Stalagmites erupted from the cavern's craggy floor. Sam frantically scanned the laboratory until he saw two bracelets lying on a keyboard beneath the huge screen where Byron Castlemaine tracked criminal activity around the city.

The bracelets were simply designed, having just two buttons. Pressing the red one caused the wearer to shrink, while the blue button restored a person to their normal size. Sam grabbed the bracelets and pulled the sketchpad and pen from his pocket. He quickly drew a picture of the interior of Baron Midnight's fortress. He included Tanya standing at the exact location where he had left her before vanishing. Sam began to add his own likeness, but before he finished, he remembered that the Speck's wristbands always had to be charged before use.

Sam walked behind the oversized screen where a stalagmite and stalactite had fused together. Embedded in the petrified column was the charger. Sam placed both bracelets inside it and pulled a lever on the side of the column. Then he recited the Speck's secret oath:

> *Where evil dwells in the midnight hour,*
> *I swear to fight with all my power.*
> *Let evildoers all take flight;*
> *The Speck shall fight the cause of right.*

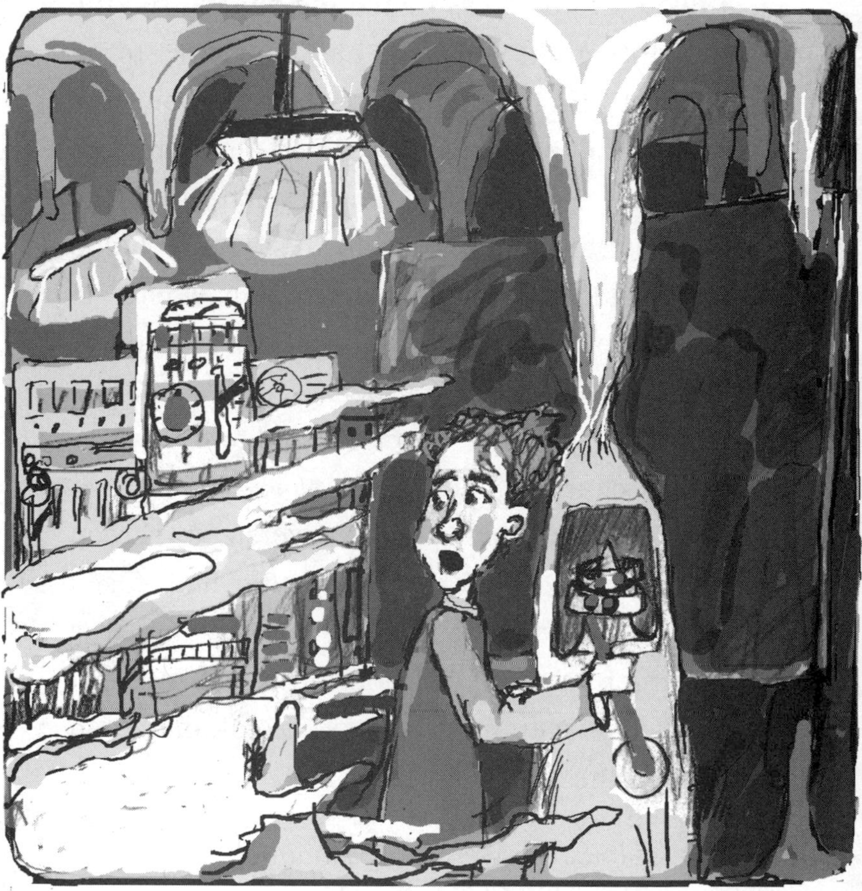

Suddenly, the cavern was bathed in a deep red light, and Sam realized he had activated Castlemaine's security system. Sam turned as he heard a low hissing sound. Pale yellow fumes began to seep into the cave. Sleeping gas! It was impossible to tell whether the bracelets were fully charged, but Sam snatched them anyway. He then grabbed his sketchpad and hurriedly completed the picture, vanishing as gas filled the laboratory.

Tanya was standing directly in front of him when Sam reappeared.

"Incredible," she murmured, shaking her head in disbelief. "You were only gone for a minute. Do you have the bracelets?"

"Yes," said Sam, tightly fastening one of them onto his left wrist and pocketing the other, "but I don't know if they're fully charged. Let's go to Skull Tower."

Skull Tower was a labyrinth of corridors. Without Tanya guiding him, Sam would have been hopelessly lost.

"Your grandfather is in there," said Tanya, opening a thick iron gate. "He's in the cell behind that door."

Sam got down on his knees to examine the laser tripwires. The intricate network of wafer-thin red beams criss-crossed the open area. There was simply no way through.

"Trip any one of those beams," Tanya reminded Sam when he stood up again, "and the alarm will sound."

"It shouldn't be a problem."

"I've got an idea how to get you both out, but you'll have to stay small to do it. I can smuggle you in my rucksack. I'll take you with me to the rebels."

"Okay, but we'll have to move quickly. I don't know how much power is left in the bracelets."

Pressing the red button on the bracelet, Sam said, "Wish me luck."

CHAPTER EIGHT

SMALL WORLD

Sam felt as if his entire body were being pulled inside out, then forced down a narrow tube at incredibly high speed. Once Sam got his bearings, he looked up at Tanya, who was now towering above him. With a wave of his tiny hand, Sam scurried underneath the beams.

Sam could now easily slip under the security grid that extended in all directions above his head. However, the paved floor presented a challenge now that he was less than two inches tall. He had to scramble across shallow valleys between the stone slabs. After negotiating the cracks in the floor, Sam finally reached the door. Although it was a tight squeeze, he managed to slip underneath the door of his grandfather's cell.

Charles Kelly was asleep on a bunk beneath the room's only window. His glasses were lying on a footstool beside a wooden tray containing the remnants of his last meal. Sam moved away from the door and stepped into the corner of the cell. Taking a deep breath, he pressed the blue button on his bracelet. Regaining his normal size, Sam went over to the bunk and gave his grandfather a gentle nudge.

"What . . . who," stammered Kelly as he awoke. "Why, Sam! But how? How did you get here? Have you been captured too?"

Sam shook his head. "I did just like you told me in your message, Granddad," he explained. "I drew a picture of myself in *The Sensational Six* comic."

"Message?" said Kelly, looking confused. "I didn't send a message."

"But you must have," Sam objected. "Maybe it was while you were under the influence of the HypnoRay?"

"How do you know about that?" Kelly asked, as he put on his glasses and straightened his thick grey hair.

"Tanya told me," said Sam, "but there really isn't time to talk, Granddad. We need to get out of here."

"How?"

"With these," said Sam, showing his grandfather the bracelets. "I took them from the Speck's underground lab. I don't know if they're fully charged, but we have to use them to get out of here."

Sam handed his grandfather the second bracelet, and Kelly snapped the device firmly into place.

"Ready?" said Sam.

Kelly looked nervous, but gave Sam a quick nod.

"Okay, on three. One, two . . ."

Sam found himself staring across the cell at a gigantic door, his grandfather beside him.

"That was awful," Kelly gasped, steadying himself against the leg of the bunk.

"Are you okay?" Sam asked him.

"I think so," replied Kelly. "I just need a second to catch my breath."

In a few moments his grandfather was ready. They slipped under the door. After making their way safely under the beams, they saw to their dismay that two guards were in the corridor, talking with Tanya.

"The guards weren't there before. Be careful," he whispered to his grandfather. They edged along the wall, moving steadily closer to Tanya. Sam saw her glance down. She had seen them! She reached into her vest pocket and pulled out a silk handkerchief. Pretending to sneeze into it, Tanya smiled sweetly at the guards.

"There's so much dust in here," she said to the guards.

Sam watched as she let the handkerchief fall to the floor. It flared out like a huge parachute as it floated over Sam and his grandfather. Kelly instinctively tried to move away, but Sam grabbed him and held him fast. The handkerchief covered them like a massive tarpaulin.

Above him, Sam heard Tanya say, "Oops!" and then, "No, it's all right, I'll get it." Then her gigantic hand gently swept up the handkerchief with Sam and Kelly tucked safely inside. Sam felt disoriented as he clung to his grandfather. He struggled to breathe as the cloth was pressed into Tanya's vest pocket.

When Tanya pulled them out, they were back in the kitchen. They found themselves on the table beside a bowl of fruit.

"I'm going to get my rucksack. I'll be back in a minute," Tanya said softly.

"Have a rest, Granddad," said Sam.

But Kelly simply stared over Sam's shoulder, wide-eyed in fear. Sam heard a savage snarl. He turned around, and a terrifying sight confronted him. It was Cole, Tanya's cat. The monstrous feline licked his lips, hissed and prepared to pounce.

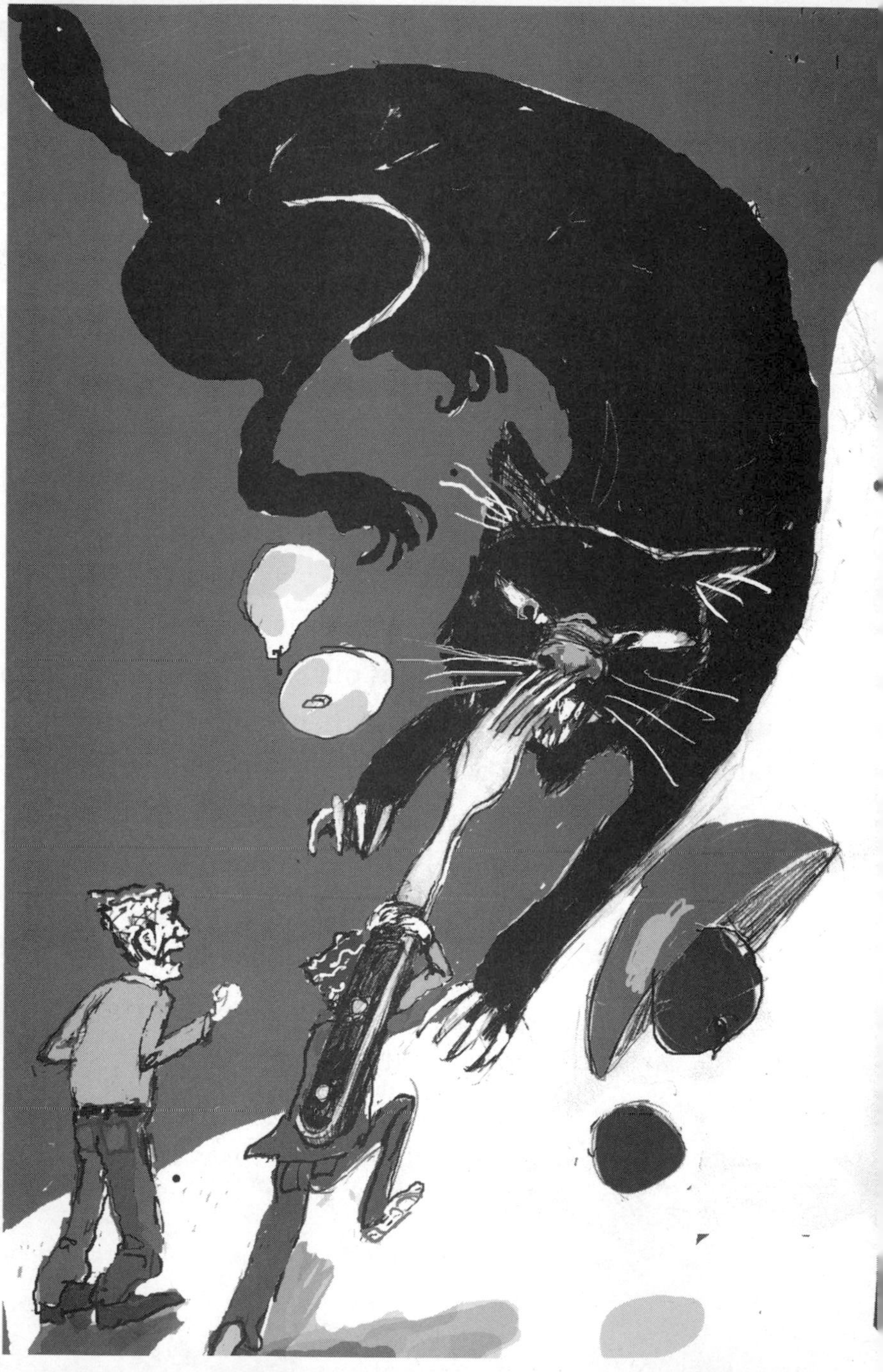

"I'll try and distract it!" yelled Sam. "Run!"

Sam waved his arms frantically, diverting the cat's attention. As it lunged, he darted aside. Then Sam noticed a fork that had been left on the table. It was huge, almost the same size as he was, but he managed to lift it. He jabbed the prongs at the cat, and it pulled back, startled. Suddenly, it swung its colossal paw at Sam, who was propelled across the length of the table. He lost his grip on the fork, and Cole crept closer, moving in for the kill. The giant cat's teeth were now clearly visible, and Sam knew he had only seconds to live.

"Cole!" Tanya yelled, rushing into the room. "You bad cat! Shoo!"

The cat leaped off the table and scurried out of the kitchen.

Kelly emerged from behind the bowl of fruit.

"Please get us out of here so we can get back to normal size," he pleaded.

"Don't worry," Tanya replied. "I just have to load some food into this rucksack, and then you can climb in. I'll tell the guards at the gate that I'm on a mission for my father."

Quickly she packed the rucksack with an assortment of fruits and vegetables, bread, sausages and a large round of Swiss cheese.

"After I put you inside, you'll be able to look out through here," she said, pointing to a small hole in the rucksack.

"I don't know how much longer we can stay this size," Sam reminded her.

"I know," Tanya agreed. "We have to move quickly."

She gently slid Sam and his grandfather into the bag. They climbed up on the round of cheese and were only just able to peer out of the hole.

"Here we go," Tanya said, hoisting the bag onto her shoulders.

She walked along the corridor and crossed the inner courtyard of the fortress, but then she abruptly stopped.

"Commander Ragnor is standing at the main gates with the sentry," she whispered, turning her head. "Stay hidden and keep quiet."

Sam gestured to his grandfather to pull farther back inside the rucksack. Sam remained where he could safely observe what was going on without being spotted.

"Good day, Lady Tanya," Sam heard Ragnor call in greeting as she approached. His voice sounded exactly as Sam had imagined it, with a sneer barely concealed below the surface. "Where are you off to?"

"I'm getting fresh information about the rebels," Tanya replied. "And I'll be staying overnight as usual."

"It could still be dangerous out there," Ragnor said.

"We have to make sure that the rebels were defeated," Tanya said. "My father would want me to get the most up-to-date information possible."

Suddenly, a voice called out. "Open the gates! The hybrids have returned!"

Sam heard the heavy gates swing open, followed by the sound of marching feet and the low growls and hissing of the hybrids as they entered the fortress. He peered out of the rucksack's hole and watched the Airserpents circling high above the inner courtyard. On the ground he saw a procession of soldiers. Some of them were dragging prisoners, bloodied remnants of the rebel army.

"You see," said Tanya. "The hybrids are utterly ruthless. They would never return if there was any danger. My father is still fighting in the Western Sector and there has been no news. I can use my contacts to get information."

"You may go," Ragnor said gruffly. "But you must report to me as soon you return."

After Tanya had walked through the main gates, she quickened her pace. When she was some distance away from the fortress, she broke into a run. The rucksack wobbled wildly, and by the time Tanya came to a halt and set it on the ground, Sam was beginning to feel seriously seasick. He was relieved when Tanya lifted him and his grandfather out and placed them on the ground.

Sam reached for the blue button on his bracelet and nodded to his grandfather to do the same. Yet neither of them had time to press their controls. Without warning, Sam and his grandfather suddenly regained their normal size. The bracelets' power had finally been exhausted. They'd made it to the safety of the woods just in time.

CHAPTER NINE

THE POISONED PEN

"That was close," said Sam, with a heavy sigh of relief.

"Is he okay?" Tanya asked, staring over at Kelly, who was leaning against a tree, holding his chest and taking deep breaths.

"He'll be fine," said Sam. "The shrinking and enlarging process is very uncomfortable, that's all."

"I'm worried that my father's forces might be returning from the Western Sector, but I can't see anything from here."

She walked over to a nearby oak. "This should do just fine," she said, beckoning to Sam, "but I'll need your help to reach the lowest branch. Hold your hands together and give me a boost."

Sam did as she asked and watched as Tanya grabbed a branch and expertly scurried up the tree. She reminded him of a spider monkey. Once she was out of sight, Sam turned to his grandfather. He took out his sketchpad and turned to the pages he had drawn in the studio. He looked at his grandfather in consternation.

"See, you did contact me," Sam insisted. "Here's the picture I drew. Look what you said," he added, pointing to a word balloon.

"It's my likeness," Kelly admitted, "but I didn't write that. How could I? I was a prisoner. I didn't have the power to do anything."

"But if it wasn't you, who was it?"

Kelly's eyes widened in horror.

"Karakor!" he gasped. "It must have been him. But why?"

"What are you talking about? I think there's a lot you're not telling me."

Kelly swallowed hard and looked down. He told Sam how he had first acquired the mysterious pen and encountered Karakor. Sam was shocked. How could the man he had idolized all his life be so deceitful and shallow?

"I wrote the story Karakor asked for," Kelly continued, "but there was no way I was going to let it be published. I spent decades producing adventures about heroes who stood for everything that was good in the world. I simply couldn't bring myself to betray that. Karakor was furious and dragged me into this world."

"A world you created," said Sam.

"Exactly, but I didn't realize that the world I'd created was a living universe with real people and real suffering. So the story I created for Karakor has brought everyone unimaginable misery. And I've got you trapped here as well. I wish I'd never touched that pen!"

"Wait a minute," declared Sam. "That's it. Maybe you can draw us out of this."

He handed his grandfather the sketchpad and pen. When Kelly tried to draw, however, Sam noticed that the jewel didn't glow.

"It's no use," said Kelly, handing him back the pad. "This is what I really draw like."

Sam couldn't believe his eyes. On the paper were two miserable stick figures in a crudely drawn forest.

Just then, Sam heard a rustling in the tree overhead. Tanya hung briefly from the lowest branch, then jumped to the ground.

"The coast is clear," she said, once she had caught her breath. "There's no sign of my father or his troops. He must still be in the Western Sector. We're safe for a while. Let's eat."

Tanya reached into her rucksack and handed Sam the bread and a small folding knife. "Slice the bread for sandwiches," she said, pulling out the cheese.

While they ate, the mood was grim. "Without the heroes, we can't hold out much longer," Tanya admitted. "Now that the rebels have shown their hand, my father will go all out to destroy what's left of them. I just hope that my cousin Altina got away safely. She was leading the assault."

Sam thought back to what he had seen during the battle.

"She's dead," he said, heavily. "I saw her under the pincers of a Scorpion."

Tanya's face drained of colour, and Sam could see her holding back tears. Sam put the folding knife into his pocket and gave her a hug.

"My cousin's death is a great loss," she said solemnly, "but we're not beaten yet. The heroes will be freed and defeat my father. Once the Sensational Six and the others are released, this nightmare will be over, and you'll be able to go back to your own world."

"You're right, Tanya," Sam said. "We've got this far. We can't give up now."

Around twilight, they arrived at a village beside a lake. The main street was lined with white-walled cottages and other buildings with thatched roofs. They stopped in front of a barn.

"Wait here," said Tanya. Then she went inside.

A few moments later, she returned, accompanied by a young man whose long hair was tied in a ponytail. Sam recognized him from the earlier battle. The man nodded quickly to Kelly and flashed a brief smile at Sam, but said nothing.

"This is my cousin Andreas," Tanya announced. "I've explained everything to him. He's going to take us to someone who can help."

They soon arrived at a small cottage at the edge of the village. Andreas knocked three times on the door, which opened slowly. An old man with stark-white hair and a bushy beard greeted them. Sam instantly recognized him as Copernicus, a wise old man who had first appeared in *Sensational Six* #17.

"Andreas!" he cried. "And Tanya. Come in, come in."

Tanya and Andreas stepped inside, and Sam and Kelly followed.

"And who are these fine people?" Copernicus asked.

Tanya quickly explained. Copernicus did not seem at all surprised to learn Sam and Kelly's identities. Sam remembered that the old man often dabbled in magic, mixing potions and casting spells. The cottage was a cluttered mess, and the kitchen table was covered in books and papers.

"So they have come to help us defeat your father?" Copernicus asked.

"Yes, if we can release the heroes from ContraRealm," Tanya said. "We need your help to work out a plan."

"Very well," Copernicus said. "Tanya, we need to talk. Sam, you and your grandfather get some rest."

"There are beds up in the loft," said Andreas, grabbing a lamp. "You'll be safe there. I'll show you the way."

CHAPTER TEN

THE RELUCTANT RETURN

When Sam and his grandfather entered the kitchen early the next morning, Tanya, Andreas and Copernicus were deep in conversation.

"So, what's the plan?" Sam asked.

"The ContraRay machine is kept in Dome Tower, next to my father's laboratory," Tanya explained. "But I'm not sure if we can use it to release the heroes."

"It will probably have to be reprogrammed," said Copernicus thoughtfully. "There must be some codes to enter. Thankfully, we have Mr. Kelly here to tell us what to do."

"I'm sorry," confessed Kelly, "but I don't know anything about any codes. I have no idea how to work the machine."

"What do you mean, you don't know?" Tanya asked, appalled.

"But, Granddad, you wrote the story," Sam said. "You must know how to use it."

"Well, when I created the story, I left it kind of vague," Kelly explained sheepishly. "My heart wasn't in it, and I didn't intend to publish the comic, after all."

"I've got it!" Sam exclaimed. "Even if you don't know the ContraRay codes, Granddad, Baron Midnight must know."

"Of course he does," said Tanya, "but he's not just going to tell us, is he?"

"You're not thinking," Sam said. "We can use the HypnoRay on him."

"It might work," said Andreas, "but it will be very risky."

"We will have to move quickly," said Copernicus. "After the recent battle in the Western Sector, our forces pulled back beyond the river.

Baron Midnight no doubt believed he had won, but this was only a strategic retreat. Our forces are already making their way along the mountain paths to circle around the baron's army. At seven o'clock tonight, the rebels will launch a surprise attack on the fortress. If the heroes are free by then, we stand a better chance of success."

"Tanya, you'll need to get the ContraRealm codes from Baron Midnight," said Andreas. "Sam, you'll need to go with her. It's too dangerous for one person."

"But how are we going to get my father to submit to the HypnoRay?"

Copernicus held up a small glass vial filled with a clear liquid. "This sleeping draught will immobilize him long enough for you to use the HypnoRay. Once you have the information, you can free the heroes."

"What about me?" Kelly asked. "Can I help?"

"I'm afraid not," said Andreas. "You would be recognized immediately, so you need to stay out of sight. You'll be perfectly safe here with Copernicus."

"Sam, you'll need to pose as someone from the village," said Copernicus. "Andreas, get him some suitable clothes."

"So, I'm going in with Tanya?" Sam asked.

"No," said Copernicus. "It's too dangerous for you to go together. Tanya can get inside without any trouble, but you must enter separately."

"But how are you going to get me inside?" asked Sam.

"We need some kind of official document," Copernicus mused. "We could forge one, but the problem is that it would still need to have Baron Midnight's signature."

"Well, I can do that!" Kelly exclaimed.

Everyone around the table stared at him.

"Sam," said Kelly, "do you remember in *Sensational Six* #4, when Baron Midnight wrote a note to Tanya while she was away at boarding school?"

"It doesn't sound familiar," Sam replied, shaking his head.

"I remember that note!" said Tanya.

"Well, who do you think wrote it?" Kelly asked. "I did! In my own handwriting."

"So Baron Midnight's handwriting must be . . ."

"Identical to mine!" Kelly declared.

"Perfect," said Sam. "We shouldn't have a problem getting into the fortress now."

"If we want you both inside the fortress before Baron Midnight returns, we have to hurry," Andreas interjected. "Our intelligence tells us that he's planning to fly back to the castle once his troops are deployed along the river. That only gives us a few hours."

"Tanya, get ready to leave. You'll be safer if you go alone," Copernicus ordered. "Andreas, you wait an hour and follow with Sam."

When he reached the main entrance to the fortress, Sam's stomach was churning. He couldn't believe he was simply going to stroll right in. He walked up to the guards at the main gate and handed them the note his grandfather had written. One of the guards quickly read it:

Admit this boy to the fortress. He is fully authorized to make a report on our progress in the Western Sector directly to Commander Ragnor.

Signed,
Baron Midnight

"Come with me," the first guard said. "I'll take you to Commander Ragnor."

Sam followed the guard across the inner courtyard, then up the steps to the upper level. At the top of the stairs, two guards nodded, then stood aside to let them through. Sam was then led along a hallway where the walls displayed antique weapons, including swords, spears, battle-axes, guillotine blades, clubs and a wide variety of ghastly torture devices. As they approached Ragnor's private quarters, the entrance door swung open, and the commander stepped out. He closed the door behind him and kept his gaze firmly fixed on Sam.

"What do you want?" he asked coldly. "Who are you, boy?"

"A messenger from Baron Midnight," Sam answered calmly.

"Then I will need to question you," said Ragnor. "Come with me. And, you!" Ragnor barked at the guard. "Go down to the kitchen and tell them to bring my dinner right now!"

Sam followed the commander into his office.

Sam was relieved to see Tanya inside Ragnor's quarters, but was careful not to acknowledge her. Ragnor sat down at his desk and turned to Tanya.

"This boy has word of your father."

"I'm anxious to hear what he has to say," said Tanya. "May I stay?"

"By all means," Ragnor said. He looked at Sam. "So, make your report."

Ragnor's cold grey eyes narrowed as he waited for Sam's response. Sam swallowed hard and recited the words he had memorized.

"The battle is going well. The rebels in the Western Sector have been driven to the far side of the river. The baron and his forces will be returning to the fortress as soon as possible."

THERE HE IS! IT'S MY FATHER!

"Excellent!" said Ragnor, as the servant arrived with his meal. "Tanya, take this boy down to the kitchen and give him something to eat."

Instead of going to the kitchen, Tanya led Sam up a nearby staircase to the top of a turret. She looked out a window, then pointed to a black dot in the distant sky.

"There he is!" Tanya cried. "It's my father! We've got to get to him before Ragnor does."

Sam peered out as the shape grew larger. It was indeed Baron Midnight's black helicopter gunship, decorated with the batwinged skull emblem. The aircraft briefly hovered above the fortress, then slowly began its descent toward the launch area. As soon as it landed, Baron Midnight stepped out and quickly swept past the guards, who scampered to keep up with him.

"We've got to move fast," Sam said, and they rushed back down the staircase.

CHAPTER ELEVEN

THE POWER OF PERSUASION

"Good evening, Father," said Tanya, as she entered Baron Midnight's living quarters with Sam.

The room was far from luxurious. The walls were bare, and the room was sparsely furnished, containing just a few small tables and chairs. The elevated ceiling was painted white and criss-crossed with dark wooden beams. Two bearskin rugs with attached heads lay across the floor directly in front of the fireplace, where a welcoming fire crackled. Baron Midnight was seated in a high-backed chair, cradling a wine goblet.

In the glow of the firelight, the chief villain of so many of Charles Kelly's tales was a formidable sight. The baron wore his black armour and red cape, but not the metal mask that hid his disfigured features. His face had been a constant source of speculation among fans of the Sensational Six's adventures. As Sam moved closer, he could see that Baron Midnight had thinning black hair and that his face was covered in hideous scars.

The baron smiled broadly at his beloved daughter as she approached. Tanya kissed him gently on the cheek in greeting.

"And who is this?" the baron asked curiously.

"This is Karl, my friend from one of the villages," Tanya replied. Then she added quickly, "Were your operations in the Western Sector successful, Father?"

"Completely," declared Baron Midnight. He drained his goblet in one gulp.

"More wine, Tanya," the baron ordered.

"At once, Father," said Tanya.

The baron then pointed at the empty chair by the fire, inviting Sam to sit down.

"So," said Baron Midnight, settling back in his chair. "You are from one of the villages?"

"Yes," Sam replied.

"Strange," said the baron, leaning closer and peering intently into Sam's face. "You look oddly familiar. Do you perhaps have family who work here at the fortress?"

Sam felt extremely uneasy. The baron's eyes were different colours. The right one was a deep blue, and the left a pale grey.

"Are you sure we have not met before? Perhaps I know your father?"

Before Sam could answer, Tanya returned. "Your wine, Father," she said, handing the baron his goblet.

"Thank you, my dear," said Baron Midnight, taking a sip.

"So," he said, returning to Sam. "I was asking about your father. You remind me of—"

The baron stopped talking in mid-sentence and collapsed backward in his chair.

"We must hurry," said Tanya. "I put the sleeping draught in the wine."

Tanya crouched down and pressed the left eye on the head of one of the bearskin rugs. On the wall beside the fireplace, a panel slid open. Tanya pulled out an object resembling a cellphone and flipped it open. Sam immediately recognized it as the HypnoRay. The device had a small screen with a row of buttons below it. Tanya selected one of the buttons, and two short antennae emerged from each side of the device, followed by a coiled antenna from a slot just above the screen. Tanya pressed a button, and a pale blue beam shot out and struck Baron Midnight's forehead. Tanya showed Sam the HypnoRay's miniature screen, where an X-ray image of the baron's skull appeared. She pressed another button, and the blue light expanded to surround her father's head. The baron's eyes opened, but he was in a trance, staring directly ahead, focusing on nothing.

"How do you work the ContraRay?" Tanya asked.

"I alone can use the machine," murmured the baron.

Tanya increased the ray's intensity.

"I alone have the touch," the baron said again.

"This is getting us nowhere," said Tanya in frustration. She prepared to increase the HypnoRay's power again.

"Wait a second," said Sam. "I have an idea."

He edged closer to Baron Midnight. "What do you mean by *the touch*?" he asked.

"I alone have the touch," repeated the baron, lifting up his right hand, which was encased in a black metal gauntlet.

Sam could see that the palm and digits of the gauntlet contained swirls and patterns resembling fingerprints.

"That's it!" Sam exclaimed. "The ContraRay must be controlled through the glove. Can we remove it without breaking him out of the trance?"

"I'll try," said Tanya.

She reached for the twin fasteners that secured the gauntlet to the sleeve of Baron Midnight's armour. She unclipped the glove, carefully easing it off her father's hand. But just then, Sam and

Tanya were startled by a beeping sound. Sam at once feared they had tripped a security alarm but then noticed a small red light steadily pulsing on the baron's other forearm.

"What is it?" he asked.

"Ragnor," replied Tanya. "He always calls around this time to confirm the evening's guard deployments. We have to answer, or he'll be suspicious."

Tanya depressed the red light.

"Good evening, Excellency," said Ragnor's voice. "What are your instructions for tonight?"

Tanya moved closer to her father and whispered in his ear.

"Tell him to make the usual arrangements," she said, before pushing the light again.

"The usual arrangements," the baron repeated in a monotone.

"As you wish," replied Ragnor.

Tanya whispered into her father's ear again.

"Dismiss the guards around the laboratory, Ragnor," instructed Baron Midnight. "I will be

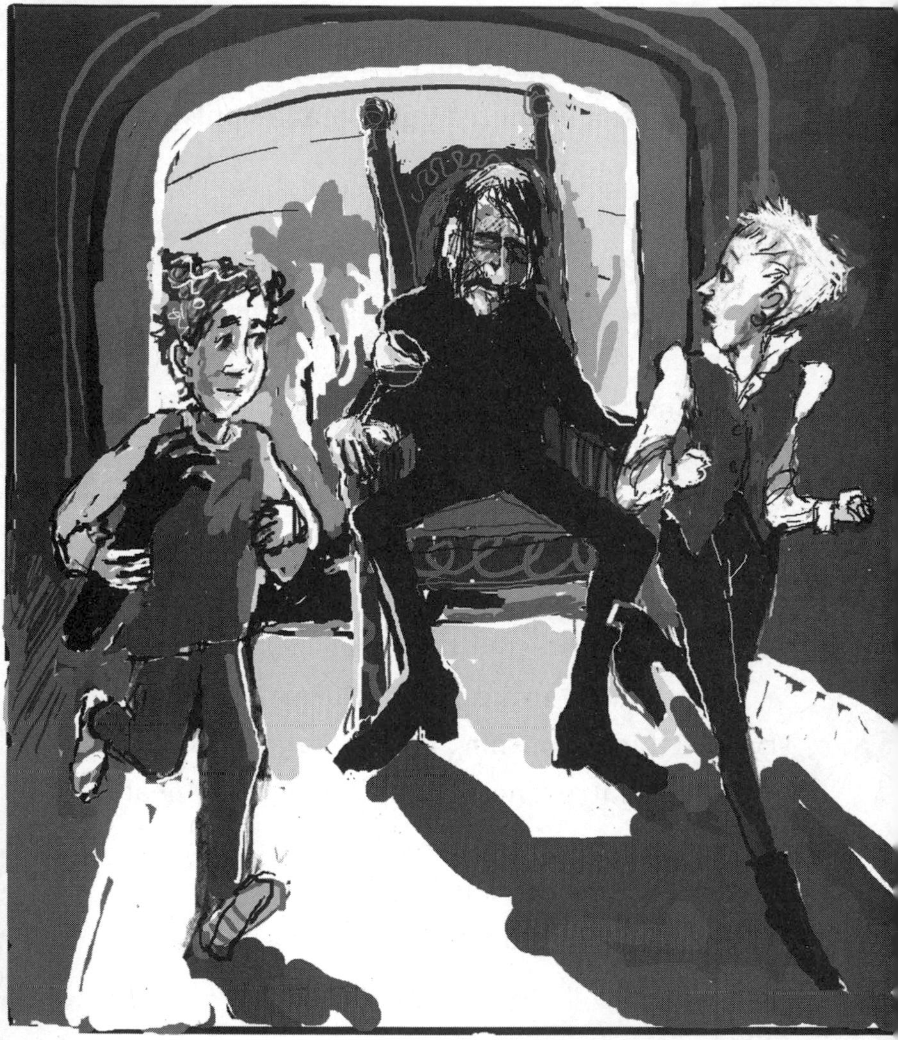

working there for most of the night, and I don't wish to be disturbed."

"At once," said Ragnor. "Good night, Excellency."

Tanya handed Baron Midnight's metal gauntlet to Sam, and then gave her father one final command. "Sleep now," she whispered.

The baron's head slowly drooped until his chin rested on his chest, and he began to snore.

"How long will he sleep?" said Sam.

"The HypnoRay usually lasts for about two hours," Tanya replied. "Let's get going. The rebels will be attacking soon."

CHAPTER TWELVE

HYBRID HORROR

Sam was apprehensive as he and Tanya made their way to the entrance to Dome Tower. At last they came to a thick steel door. Tanya quickly punched a numeric code into a small keypad on the adjacent wall, and the door swung open.

Baron Midnight's laboratory was a large room surrounded by stone walls. Along the walls were tall tubes filled with clear liquid.

"After the hybrids are created, those tubes are where they are first grown," said Tanya.

"Why are they all empty?" Sam asked her.

Tanya didn't reply. Instead she simply raised her eyes in the direction of the vaulted ceiling, shrouded in shadows. Peering up into the gloom, Sam was shocked at what he saw. Suspended high above him were at least fifty embryonic sacs. Sam shuddered at the squelching sound as some of the nightmarish creatures wriggled and squirmed in their cocoons.

"Those are Wolfbats," Tanya told him.

"I don't remember *them!*"

"They're new," Tanya explained. "They have a wolf's body, strong jaws and razor-sharp teeth and claws. They also possess the leathery wings of bats, so they have the power of flight."

Beyond the baron's laboratory was another much larger room. Sam and Tanya cautiously made their way inside.

The room was dominated by an enormous machine resembling a huge telescope, which was set at a ninety-degree angle to the ceiling. Sam assumed the dome's ceiling was designed to slide partially open to allow the machine to access the sky. The entire apparatus rested on a platform that enabled it to swivel and rise.

Sam walked over to the machine and saw a hand imprint in the centre of its upper panel.

This must be the control mechanism, he thought.

He slipped on the gauntlet and cautiously inserted it into the opening. It was a perfect fit. Suddenly, the air was filled with the low hum of the ContraRay. The dome's ceiling was steadily transformed until it displayed a vast canopy containing thousands of stars sprinkled across a background of inky blackness. Suddenly the scene changed and Sam watched as the petrified forms of the Sensational Six and all of Charles Kelly's other superhero characters appeared high above him.

The indestructible Titan had been halted in mid-attack, his huge fists still raised high over his head, a look of unbridled fury on his face. SynthoLord the android's expression was simply blank. Golden Guardian and Redhawk seemed to have been plucked from the sky. Supernova was frozen next to them, her flame powers completely extinguished. To her right, Psychic Girl was also immobilized. Behind them Sam could see a small army of Charles Kelly characters. The Speck must have been there somewhere but was too tiny to see.

"Good evening, Baron Midnight," said a voice.

"Commence deactivation procedure!" Sam ordered.

I hope this works, he thought.

"Deactivation will result in all current inhabitants of ContraRealm returning to your world. Do you still wish to proceed?"

"I do," said Sam.

"Deactivation procedure initiated."

The controls on both sides of the hand imprint became illuminated, and a lengthy series of numbers began counting down.

"It's working," said Tanya.

"How long will it take?" Sam asked her.

Before Tanya could answer, a crashing sound from the adjoining room made them both whirl around. One of the overhead sacs had ruptured,

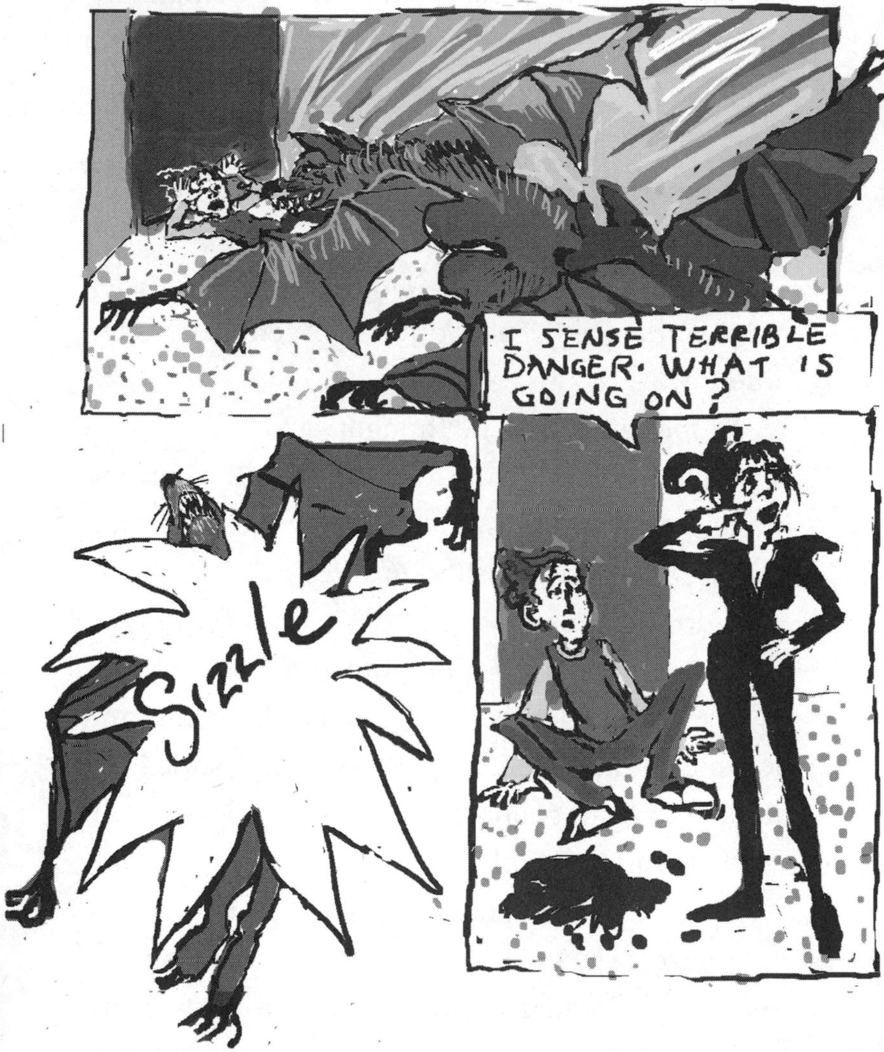
I SENSE TERRIBLE DANGER. WHAT IS GOING ON?
Sizzle

and a Wolfbat lay squirming on the laboratory floor in a large puddle of liquid.

"We have to get out," said Tanya.

"But the heroes aren't free yet," Sam protested.

"We can't wait!" Tanya snapped. "The other Wolfbats will be maturing any minute. Look!"

She pointed toward the ceiling, where the remaining cocoons were steadily leaking and beginning to tear open.

"Let's go!" Tanya yelled.

Sam was right behind her as Tanya sprinted out of the room and across the laboratory floor. But before they could reach the exit, a Wolfbat swooped down on them, screeching and snarling. Sam was knocked flat on his back. He looked up to see the creature bearing down on him with its jaws open wide.

Suddenly, a ball of fire slammed into the Wolfbat, incinerating it instantly. Supernova was now free and was using her flame power to blast the emerging hybrids. Behind her, Sam saw the other heroes bursting out of ContraRealm and joining the battle. The Titan easily smashed any Wolfbats in his path, while SynthoLord simply brushed the monsters aside. To Sam it was like a fantastic dream, but it was really happening. All of his favourite superheroes were right there in front of him.

The fighting was furious, but was over almost before it began, although a handful of Wolfbats managed to escape through the shattered roof. As soon as the battle was over, the flames encompassing Supernova's body quickly disappeared as she assumed her human form.

"Tanya, we owe you our lives," she said. She was then joined by the other members of the Sensational Six.

"And who is this, Tanya?" Psychic Girl asked, looking with intense curiosity at Sam.

"This is just a friend from the village," answered Tanya, quickly changing the subject. She explained everything that had happened and warned the heroes about the impending rebel assault.

"In that case," said Golden Guardian. "It looks like things are about to get rough around here. You two need to be taken to safety."

CHAPTER THIRTEEN

SUNSET FOR MIDNIGHT

It was almost seven o'clock as Sam and Tanya hurried to keep up with the imperious figure of Baron Midnight. They walked confidently through the inner courtyard of the fortress toward the baron's helicopter gunship. As they approached the aircraft, the surrounding guards saluted.

"Excellency," the head guard stammered. "We didn't expect you."

"Out of my way!" the baron snapped.

Sam smiled as the guards ushered the three of them into the gunship. Baron Midnight slammed the door and started the engine. The helicopter rose into the air. When they were high above the castle, the form of Baron Midnight changed. There in his place in the pilot's seat was SynthoLord, the shape-shifting android.

"Our timing was precise," the android said. "The battle has begun."

Sam and Tanya peered out of the windows. As planned, the rebel army was attacking in force. Ragnor was mobilizing his troops, and the hybrids were grouping for a counter-attack. Sam could see the commander saluting as the helicopter hovered above the fortress.

At that moment, the heroes emerged from Dome Tower. Looking down, Sam could see the Titan racing out and slamming Crocbears. Psychic Girl employed her mental powers to lift the weapons from Baron Midnight's soldiers' hands. Simultaneously, she aimed one arm toward the hovering helicopter, enveloping it in a flash of light.

"Psychic Girl has placed an invisible energy shield around us," SynthoLord explained. "We can watch the battle in safety now."

"Look! It's my father," Tanya exclaimed.

Baron Midnight was now wearing his familiar black metal mask. They watched as the baron staggered toward Ragnor and pointed frantically toward the gunship. Ragnor immediately aimed his blaster at the helicopter, but its deadly ray bounced harmlessly off the transparent shield that Psychic Girl had erected.

All around them, Sam could see the airborne hybrids as they fought the flying superheroes. He heard the piercing shrieks of the dying creatures, followed by a series of short explosions. He saw the flaming figure of Supernova soaring in the sky, hurling balls of flame at the Wolfbats, sending them plunging to the ground below. Redhawk, his feathered wings illuminated by the setting sun, swooped in to attack. Above the trees, Golden Guardian flew directly at the fleeing Airserpents, blasting them to smithereens. He then roared toward the Waspillas, quickly destroying them, but dozens of others swarmed around him. Seeing her leader in danger, Supernova broke off from her battle with the Wolfbats and flew down to aid

Golden Guardian. She fired volleys of fireballs at the enraged Waspillas. This gave Golden Guardian a chance to recover, and, between them, the two heroes made short work of the repulsive creatures.

They turned their attention toward the remaining Wolfbats. Redhawk was not finding them easy targets, but was steadily gaining the upper hand. Supernova was able to fling an occasional fireball toward a Scorplion that was in battle with the Titan below. Although it briefly pinned him to the ground with its deadly stinger poised to strike, the Titan managed to pull its pincers apart and deliver a knockout blow to the savage monster.

Sam's attention was diverted by the sound of a tremendous explosion. In the distance, he could see that the northern wall of the fortress had been breached. The rebel forces streamed in.

As the tide turned decisively against Baron Midnight, Sam noticed Ragnor running toward the forest. At that moment, however, Supernova flung a fireball at the last of the Wolfbats,

setting its right wing ablaze. The hybrid went into a tailspin and collided with the escaping Ragnor. The commander tried to scream, but the enraged Wolfbat snapped its jaws around Ragnor's neck, silencing him forever. Still gripping the commander's lifeless form, the hybrid shot back up into the air, before a final blast from Supernova sent it crashing into the mountainside in a ball of fire.

Sam could see that the fighting within the fortress was going well. Charles Kelly's other heroes were easily mopping up the remaining soldiers. The rebels had secured the compound.

Baron Midnight himself was in a desperate struggle. On top of the wall above the main gates of the fortress, the baron and Golden Guardian were locked in battle as high-powered energy beams shot out from their palms. In the comics, Baron Midnight had always fought the Sensational Six to a mutually exhausting draw, but this time Sam was certain that the baron was doomed to defeat. Suddenly, the blasters in the baron's palms stopped firing, and he tottered from side to side.

Golden Guardian fired a final blast, and Baron Midnight fell headlong off the fortress wall.

Sam looked over at Tanya and saw tears streaming down her face.

"It's over," she whispered to herself as the helicopter sped off toward the lake.

CHAPTER FOURTEEN

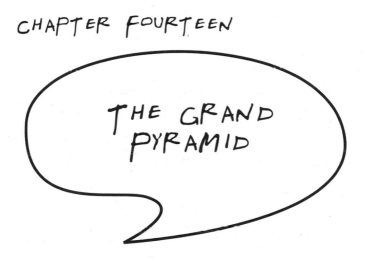

THE GRAND PYRAMID

The next morning when Sam awoke, he was once again in the loft of Copernicus' cottage.

"Get up, Sam," Kelly said. "You have to get us back home."

"What?" Sam asked, groggily.

"There's no reason for us to stick around," said his grandfather. "The heroes are free, and Baron Midnight has been defeated. You can use the pen to draw us back into my studio. It's time for us to leave."

"I guess you're right," Sam replied, "but first, we have to say goodbye to everyone."

When they went downstairs, Tanya, Andreas and Copernicus were sitting at the kitchen table, drinking coffee.

"Good morning, my friends," Copernicus greeted them. "Come have some breakfast."

"I just got back from the fortress," said Andreas, as Sam and Kelly took their seats at the table.

"Is Baron Midnight dead?" Sam asked.

"No," said Andreas. "Miraculously, he was found unconscious beside the fortress wall. He's been placed in the same cell where you were kept, Mr. Kelly."

"Death would have been too good for that tyrant," said Kelly, taking a sip from his coffee.

"We couldn't have beaten him without your help," said Andreas.

"But I'm to blame for what's happened to all of you," Kelly said, mournfully. "If it wasn't for me—"

"If it wasn't for you, none of us would even exist," Copernicus interrupted. "You are our creator. We owe our very existence to you."

"I have an announcement," Sam said. "I think it's time we went back home."

Tanya looked at him with sadness.

"I knew this day would come. I will miss you both."

"What about you?" Sam asked her.

"You needn't worry about me," Tanya assured him. "I'll be quite safe. Now that my father has been defeated, this world must be rebuilt."

After they had finished breakfast, Sam shook hands with Andreas and Copernicus and gave Tanya a hug. Sam couldn't imagine how his grandfather felt, being face to face with the creations of his own imagination.

"It's been an honour," Kelly said, as he gave each of them a hug. Sam could see a tear fall from his grandfather's eye.

Sam took out his pad and the pen. He thought for a moment, and then drew a sketch of the attic studio from memory, inserting himself and his grandfather into the drawing. But the gemstone failed to glow. Although Sam rubbed it with his thumb, nothing happened.

"Maybe it only works when you draw something from your grandfather's stories," Tanya suggested

"Wait a minute," declared Sam. "That's it. Granddad, do you remember *The Sword of Borak?*"

"Not very well," Kelly confessed, with a shrug. "It only ran for a short time."

"Nine issues in total," confirmed Sam, "but in the last one, the evil warlock Velaron secured a magical emerald called the Heart of Alcarus. It was a portal to all possible universes."

"I don't follow," said Kelly, shaking his head.

"Think about it, Granddad," Sam continued. "I took the Speck's bracelets from his lab and used them to free you. If we can travel into that Borak story, we may be able to use the Heart of Alcarus to get home."

"Okay," said Kelly, "but you know there's no guarantee that it will work."

"It's worth a try," said Sam. He thought hard for a moment. He recalled that Velaron's stronghold was deep within a massive pyramid in the ancient coastal city of Taraxica. Quickly, Sam drew a panel from *The Sword of Borak* depicting the Grand Pyramid's inner chamber.

Once he had placed himself and his grandfather in the illustration, the emerald glowed brightly.

"Goodbye, Sam. Goodbye, Mr. Kelly," said Tanya with a smile. "It was wonderful to meet you."

Sam smiled back at her, touched the jewel with his thumb, and the room disappeared.

CHAPTER FIFTEEN

INTO THE HEART

Sam and Kelly found themselves in semi-darkness at the perimeter of the pyramid's inner chamber. They quickly hid behind a massive marble statue of one of the legendary gods of Taraxica. Sam cautiously peered around it, waiting for his eyes to adjust to the dim light. At the far end of the chamber, flaming torches illuminated a small group of white-robed men and women kneeling in a semicircle. They were chanting softly in front of a gigantic green gemstone. It was the Heart of Alcarus. It stood on a platform surrounded by marble columns. Sam could remember it from the comics. The emerald was pulsing gently, bathing the entire inner chamber in a pale green glow.

"What's going on?" asked Kelly, at Sam's shoulder.

"It doesn't look as if the portal has been opened yet," Sam told him. Then the chanting suddenly ceased. "Wait a second, though. Something's happening."

The inner chamber became deathly silent. Then a hooded figure dressed in a blood-red robe and carrying a long wooden staff entered and stepped onto the platform.

Velaron stood before his minions and lowered his hood. His long, thin face was framed by black shoulder-length hair, and his beard almost reached his waist. Turning to face the Heart of Alcarus, Velaron whispered an incantation, and then stamped his staff three times. The emerald burst into life and glowed brightly as random scenes from thousands of worlds flashed rapidly across its surface.

"We need to get closer to the Heart," said Kelly.

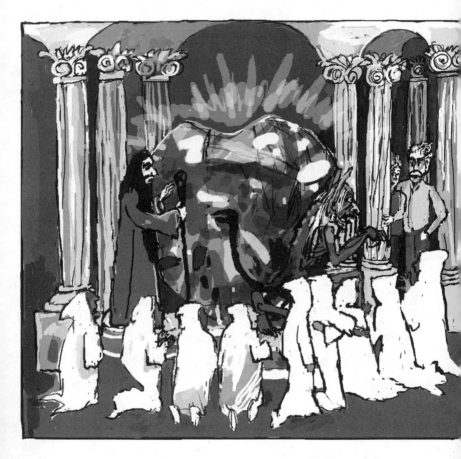

With his grandfather right behind him, Sam crept gingerly along the edge of the chamber, taking care to stay out of sight behind the columns. By the time they got as close to the platform as they dared, the images inside the Heart of Alcarus had changed to show only scenes from the real world.

Sam was about to tell his grandfather to run, when the pen in his pocket suddenly started to vibrate. Quickly, Sam reached into his pocket and pulled out the pen. The jewel was pulsating wildly. Suddenly, a blinding flash of light erupted, consuming the chamber. Velaron and his assistants were completely frozen.

"Charles Kelly," said a sinister voice. "My old friend."

Sam and his grandfather stepped out from behind a column. Standing in front of the portal was a grey-skinned demon, with yellow eyes, pointed ears and long, unkempt, white hair. His tail was at least four feet long.

"Karakor!" Kelly exclaimed.

Sam and his grandfather backed away into the chamber. But Karakor leaped onto the platform, barring their path to the Heart of Alcarus.

"How very kind of you to show me the way out," he sneered.

"I wondered why you didn't just kill me," said Kelly.

"I needed you," confessed Karakor, "but when I dragged you into this world you didn't bring the pen. Then when your grandson picked it up in the studio, I saw my chance."

When Karakor smiled, he revealed deadly vampire-like fangs.

"So it was you who sent me those messages through the sketchpad," said Sam.

"It certainly was," grinned Karakor. "I knew you wouldn't be able to resist trying to save your grandfather."

"You were in the jewel on the pen all along," said Sam.

"Of course, you fool!" Karakor replied. "I have been trapped inside that jewel for an eternity waiting for my chance. I have been watching you, until you led me here."

"The one place containing a doorway to our world," said Kelly.

"Precisely!" Karakor declared. "Now I can finally escape, and you can take my place here in my prison until you die. Now give me the pen."

"Why do you need the pen?" Kelly asked.

Karakor didn't respond.

That's the key! Sam realized. *He must need to combine the Heart of Alcarus with the gemstone on the pen to open the portal*

"Granddad," Sam whispered. "Keep him talking."

"I'm not giving you anything," Kelly said. "In fact, I would urge you to look around."

"Do you think you can fool me with that old trick?"

A fierce battle cry pierced the chamber. Karakor whirled around. Borak the Warrior rushed in, followed by twelve men brandishing swords and battle-axes.

It was the moment that Sam was waiting for. He swiftly took the small folding knife from his pocket and hurriedly pried the jewel from the barrel of the pen. Then he slipped the pen into Kelly's hand.

The demon easily dealt with Borak and his men, killing some and instantly freezing others. Borak himself was suspended in mid-leap as he flung himself at Karakor with his sword drawn.

"Kelly!" Karakor barked as he turned back to the old man. "I was simply going to abandon you here, but now I think I will enjoy killing both of you, very slowly."

"No need for that," Kelly said. "You want the pen? Here it is." He threw it at the demon, who snatched it from the air.

At that same moment, Sam grabbed Kelly's wrist and raced toward the Heart of Alcarus. In his other hand, he held the glowing jewel. Karakor roared with fury. But he was too late. Seconds before they would have been frozen solid, Sam and his grandfather were sucked into the swirling green vortex.

CHAPTER SIXTEEN

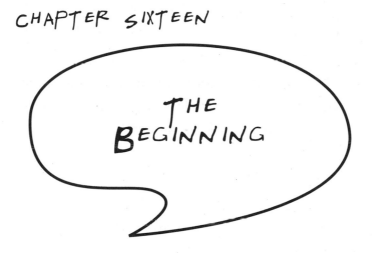

Sam lifted himself off the attic floor and looked around. His grandfather's desk had changed and was now very untidy. There was even a full cup of coffee beside the pencil sharpener. The desk calendar was still open at August 15 but now showed the current year. On the wall beside the desk was a framed photograph showing his grandfather's retirement party.

What's going on? Sam thought.

Sam decided to search for the comic that his grandfather had produced for Karakor, but it was nowhere to be seen. He pulled out his sketchpad and frantically flipped over the pages. All the illustrations he had done were still there, and the gemstone was still in his hand.

Then Sam saw a small envelope with his name on it. He tore the envelope open and read the enclosed note in astonishment.

Sam,

I hope this note finds you well. Don't be too shocked at what has happened. We were separated and emerged at different times when we passed through the Heart of Alcarus. I'll explain everything.

Granddad

Sam walked downstairs and out to the patio. He saw his parents and the Nelsons chatting. To his amazement, his grandfather was also there, sipping a glass of wine.

"You know, I never understood why you quit drawing your comics two years ago," Mr. Nelson said.

"Well, it's a funny thing," Kelly explained. "I lost my favourite pen, and I just knew it was time to quit."

Sam stared at his grandfather, who winked at him. "I think it's time for my evening stroll," said Kelly, standing up. "Would you like to join me, Sam?"

Sam nodded.

"We'll take a walk out on the old pier."

"Don't be too long, Dad," Sam's mother said. "We're about to cut your birthday cake."

As they walked, Kelly explained what had happened to him. "When I got back," he said, "I discovered that I had been returned to the exact point in time when Karakor had pulled me into the comic world."

"So I was returned to my own starting point as well," said Sam.

"Exactly," Kelly replied. "I knew you'd be confused when you appeared back in the studio, so I left you a note."

"So I guess you didn't write any more comics," Sam said.

"Without the pen, I had nothing," Kelly replied. "So I simply retired. Now we have to get rid of that emerald."

"I know," said Sam, opening his hand and examining the gemstone.

Together they walked out along the pier that stretched out sixty feet into the ocean. When they got to the end of the pier, Kelly said, "Throw it in, Sam. Let's end this story forever."

Sam flung the jewel as far as he could into the sea.

"I have an idea," Kelly said.

"What's that, Granddad?"

"Your drawings are fabulous, Sam. You have real talent, where I had none. I think together we could create even more adventures for the Sensational Six."

"That's a great idea, Granddad," Sam said. "But for now isn't it time we got back for that birthday cake?"

Also by Simon Rose

The Clone Conspiracy

"Smart kids outwit evil scientists in this science fiction thriller dealing with clones, inplanted embryos and personality downloads. As long as they realize this science *is* fiction, kids can enjoy the fast-paced action...each chapter a real cliff-hanger."

—*Victoria Times Colonist*

•

The Sorcerer's Letterbox

"As with the best timeslip fantasy, the author's obvious zest for interesting historical detail is transformed into both a compelling story and an exciting adventure ... a delightful book, and one that has a rightful place in every library in the country."

—*University of Manitoba CM Magazine*

•

The Alchemist's Portrait

"*The Alchemist's Portrait* is guaranteed to keep junior readers in suspense. Its fast paced plot will keep them reading to the end."

—*Resource Links*